Amy Cross is the author of more than 250 horror, paranormal, fantasy and thriller novels.

OTHER TITLES BY AMY CROSS INCLUDE

1689
American Coven
Angel
Anna's Sister
Annie's Room
Asylum
B&B
Bad News
The Curse of the Langfords
Daisy
The Devil, the Witch and the Whore
Devil's Briar
Eli's Town
Escape From Hotel Necro
The Farm
Grave Girl
The Haunting of Blackwych Grange
The Haunting of Nelson Street
The House Where She Died
I Married a Serial Killer
Little Miss Dead
Mary
One Star
Perfect Little Monsters & Other Stories
Stephen
The Soul Auction
Trill
Ward Z
Wax
You Should Have Seen Her

LITTLE MISS DEAD

THE HORRORS OF SOBOLTON BOOK ONE

AMY CROSS

This edition
first published by Blackwych Books Ltd
United Kingdom, 2024

Copyright © 2024 Blackwych Books Ltd

All rights reserved. This book is a work of fiction.
Names, characters, places, incidents and businesses are
the product of the author's imagination or are
used fictitiously. Any resemblance to actual persons,
living or dead, or to actual events or locations,
is entirely coincidental.

Also available in e-book format.

www.blackwychbooks.com

CONTENTS

CHAPTER ONE
page 15

CHAPTER TWO
page 25

CHAPTER THREE
page 33

CHAPTER FOUR
page 43

CHAPTER FIVE
page 51

CHAPTER SIX
page 59

CHAPTER SEVEN
page 67

CHAPTER EIGHT
page 75

CHAPTER NINE
page 83

CHAPTER TEN
page 91

CHAPTER ELEVEN
page 99

CHAPTER TWELVE
page 109

CHAPTER THIRTEEN
page 117

CHAPTER FOURTEEN
page 125

CHAPTER FIFTEEN
page 133

CHAPTER SIXTEEN
page 141

CHAPTER SEVENTEEN
page 149

CHAPTER EIGHTEEN
page 157

CHAPTER NINETEEN
page 165

CHAPTER TWENTY
page 173

CHAPTER TWENTY-ONE
page 181

CHAPTER TWENTY-TWO
page 189

CHAPTER TWENTY-THREE
page 197

CHAPTER TWENTY-FOUR
page 205

CHAPTER TWENTY-FIVE
page 213

CHAPTER TWENTY-SIX
page 221

CHAPTER TWENTY-SEVEN
page 229

CHAPTER TWENTY-EIGHT
page 237

CHAPTER TWENTY-NINE
page 245

CHAPTER THIRTY
page 253

LITTLE MISS DEAD

CHAPTER ONE

A FESTERING MASS OF human effluent sat rumbling and bubbling, packed into more than fifteen feet of intestinal tract. Wrapped around this bag of mess were numerous organs and veins, protected in some places by ribs and other bones; around this in turn was a varying layer of fat, sitting tight beneath several kilograms of blotchy skin with hair growing in places and patches of dry scales. And around this skin sat cotton and other fabrics, and pinned to one section of the fabric there was a name badge identifying the human individual generally recognized by other people as Sheriff Joseph Hicks.

Former Sheriff Joseph Hicks.

"Now, let me explain one other thing before

I get out of your way," Hicks continued. "As the new sheriff of Sobolton, you're gonna find -"

Before he could finish, he let out a sudden involuntary burp, accompanied by the sound of his large, swollen belly rumbling sympathetically. Reaching down, he winced as he used one hand to gently massage the side of his stomach.

"Sorry about that," he said with an awkward, slightly pained smile. "Gas. Must've been that chili from last night. My wife's a good cook, but these days -"

Again he burped, and this time he felt several flecks of spittle on his lips; he reached up and wiped those away, before pausing as a sensation of heartburn brought fresh pain to his already tight and uncomfortable chest. At the same time, he was trying – and mostly managing – to hold in gas at the other end.

"You're gonna find," he said after a few more seconds, wiping sweat from his brow, "that the people here require a human connection. Sobolton's a good old town, and there are about thirty thousand folks living in its boundaries and the overall county and whatnot, which can feel like a lot. Don't feel bad or like a failure if it takes you quite some time to get used to it all, but... the people wouldn't have picked you if they didn't think you were the right man for the job. Just remember that fact in your moments of doubt, John. Remember that an awful lot of people backed you."

"I won't forget that," John Tench replied, sitting uncomfortably in the opposite chair, which was already too tight and too low for him; not that he felt he could complain. "I'm honored to be given the chance to serve the people of Sobolton, and I can assure you that I will work tirelessly to keep everyone safe. This is a beautiful place, and it needs to be *kept* beautiful."

"The previous... unpleasantness... has left a bad taste," Hicks continued, adjusting his collar. "A perception of corruption's not a good thing, I see that now. We had to have a good clear-out, which is what led to the slightly unusual situation of the people wanting an outsider to come to Sobolton and take control. Now, I recognize that I might not have kept a tight grip on things before, but I honestly believe..."

He glanced around, as if he was worried that someone might overhear, and then he leaned forward a little and lowered his voice to a conspiratorial hush.

"I honestly believe," he continued, a little more softly than before, "that some of the accusations against my former deputies were unfounded and mean-spirited. There were some scores being settled, and a few local folks took the opportunity to twist the knife, but that's by the by. We've all agreed to move on, and you Mr. Tench are supposed to represent a fresh start. Now, I've cooperated with the investigation into what's gone on in this department and I'll continue to cooperate, but I agree with those that say we have to look to the future."

As his stomach rumbled again, Hicks reached a slightly swollen hand across the desk for John to shake.

"It's in that spirit, John, that I wish you all the best in your new role as sheriff of Sobolton."

***

"It's been a quiet morning so far," Carolyn said, looking down at the register she was supposed to use for recording phone calls. "Mrs. Averbury's cat has gone missing again, although 'missing' would be stretching things a little. I told her it's quite normal for cats to go out for two, three nights at a time before coming home."

"Plus this wouldn't be the first time that critter's gone wondering off," Hicks said, turning to John with a red-faced chuckle. "Approximately half the calls we get at this station are things like that. Carolyn logs them, of course, because she's obliged to do so, but she and I have an understanding that she won't bother me with the details of any unimportant calls."

"I have a black logbook," Carolyn said, sounding distinctly bored, "and a white logbook. Sheriff Hicks only looks at the white logbook. The black one just gets... filed in a drawer."

"Well," John replied, somewhat taken aback by this approach, "I think from now on, if it's alright, I'd like to have everything just go into the one logbook, and then I'll go through it and decide what's important."

"You seriously want to do that?" Carolyn asked, raisin a skeptical eyebrow.

"I just think it might be a better system," John continued. "I might notice something that's important."

"You don't think *I'd* notice if something's important?" she asked, seemingly slightly offended by his suggestion.

"I wouldn't doubt you for one second," John replied, trying to choose his words with great care. "It's just that I'd like to get a... broad view of what's going on in the area, and I think for that to happen, it'd be useful for me to know everything that's being reported. Even things that seem unimportant might help me with the process of gaining that..."

Already he could see that Carolyn was unimpressed.

"Broad view," he added again, cautiously.

Next to him, Hicks let out another loud burp, followed by a mumbled apology as he wiped his lips and then dabbed some sweat from his forehead.

"Whatever you want," Carolyn told John, taking the black logbook and making a show of dropping it into the wastepaper basket next to her desk. "After all, you're the boss."

"Well, you don't have to literally throw it away," John told her. "You can... hang onto it."

"For what purpose, Sir?" she asked, putting a little extra emphasis on that last word.

"I don't know. How much of it has been filled up?"

"Almost none," she replied. "It's a new one. The old one was full, so I started a new one on Friday and today's Monday, so there's barely anything in the new one except the lines I spent some time drawing in for the columns."

"Well, then it seems like a waste to just throw it away," John pointed out. "What happened to the old logbook that was full?"

"I burned it."

"You burned it?"

"Seemed like the best move," she told him, "but I can totally not do that in future."

"I think not burning the logbooks would be a good move," he suggested.

"I'm just following orders," she said, keeping her gaze fixed on him. "I think stability is very important, Sir, and I'm a stickler for following the rules. That's why I'm pretty much the only person being kept on after the... shall we say, scandal?"

"Excuse me," Hicks gasped, turning and hurrying off toward the bathroom, waddling slightly as if he was having slight trouble with his legs. "Be right back!"

His stomach grumbled louder than ever as he pushed the door open and disappeared from view, leaving John and Carolyn standing for a few seconds in awkward silence.

"Let me guess," she said finally, "he told you it's his wife's chili."

John turned to her.

"That's what he always tells people," she continued, with a sense of wonder in her voice, "but I don't buy it. For one thing, how often does Loretta cook chili? Every night? No way, that's just beyond belief. Of course, I haven't seen her lately to ask her, but I highly doubt that she's making the same dinner every night. For another thing, if it's having such a dramatic effect on his digestive tract, why wouldn't he ask her to ease off? And third, I don't think hot chili would have such an overwhelming impact, it just couldn't do so many horrible things to one man. Whatever's wrong with him, it seems to be a much more extensive problem that involves some more fundamental problems, and it's been going on for almost a year now." She paused, still staring up at John. "So, no," she added finally, "it's not the chili."

"Good to know," John replied, feeling as if he'd been given too much information already and wondering whether the old logbook system might in fact be better.

Before he could say anything, however, the phone on Carolyn's desk began to ring.

"He'll be a while," she added as she answered, nodding toward the bathroom door. "I wouldn't expect to see him again for at least twenty minutes. Sometimes he doesn't surface again 'til lunchtime."

"I see," John said, turning to look around the reception area as Carolyn spoke to whoever was on the other end of the line. "I'll keep that in mind."

Wandering to the opposite wall, he saw

various photos of the local area, an area that he still didn't know too well. One photo showed an old building, with a caption identifying this as a place called Middleford Cross, although someone had used a pencil to cross out that name and replace it with the word Overflow; another photo showed what appeared to be a railroad line running directly through a cemetery, while another depicted the dark main street lit up by some kind of neon-covered ice cream parlor. As he looked at more and more of these photos, he felt as if he was seeing disparate parts that somehow failed to quite connect. Could all of these places really be part of Sobolton?

"Sheriff Tench?" Carolyn said suddenly, her voice sounding a lot more tense now.

He turned and saw that she was still holding the phone, but that her entire countenance had changed and she looked distinctly worried.

"Sheriff Tench," she continued, "we've just got a report in. Someone's found the body of a young girl out at Drifter's Lake."

CHAPTER TWO

"HE'S JUST NOT BEEN himself," Norman said with a resigned tone to his voice as he looked down at the examination table. "He's been off his food, he's been acting all weird and his stool... I've noticed a distinct change to the pattern and consistency of his stool. Something's not right with him."

"Well," Lisa replied, staring down at Bruce the guinea pig, who so far was sitting obediently on the table and showing no signs of distress, "from my cursory exam I can't really find anything obviously wrong with him. His temperature's fine, his vital signs all seem good and he took some food when I offered it to him."

"But you don't *know* him," Norman pointed

out. "You don't know his quirks and idiosyncrasies."

"That's very true," Lisa admitted, although she was somewhat at a loss for words as the guinea pig continued to merely do nothing remarkable on the table between them. "I can keep him in for observation, Norman, if that would put your mind at rest. Of course, you'd be incurring a cost that I really don't think is necessary, so I'd be happier if you took him home and monitored him, and then in a few days -"

"I'd like him to stay in for observation," he told her.

"As I mentioned, there's a cost for that," she explained, "and your pet insurance -"

"I don't care about any of that," he replied, interrupting her yet again. "When my wife died last year, she made me promise to look after Bruce, and I'm not a man who breaks his promises."

"Of course not."

"I want him to have the very best," he continued, struggling to hold back tears. "If I have to sell a few things to cover the cost, then so be it, but damn it he will not suffer!" He reached up and wiped a few of the first tears away, and then he took a checkbook from the inside pocket of his coat. "Mary-Ann's looking down on us, and if I don't do right by Bruce, she'll come back and haunt me."

"I'm sure she wouldn't."

"Oh, she told me she would," he replied earnestly. "She couldn't be clearer about that. She told me not to worry about her haunting me after she was gone, she said she wouldn't do that, not unless I broke my promise to look after Bruce. Then, she told me, she'd rain hellfire down upon my soul, and Mary-Ann wasn't a woman given to idle threats. So if you don't mind, Doctor Sondnes, I really *need* to do the right thing." He looked up at the ceiling, as if he expected to see some kind of avenging angel appear at any moment. "I just can't take the risk."

He opened the checkbook and took a pen from another pocket. His hand was trembling as he began to fill out some details.

"If you don't mind," he added, "would you be okay with not cashing this until the end of the week? You'd be saving me having to... move some money around."

"Let me see what I can do," Lisa said after a moment. "I'll ask Rachel to shift a few items in the computer, and we can probably give Bruce a night's room and board for free. No need to bother your insurance people or incur any unnecessary costs."

"You'd do that for us?" Norman replied, looking at her again as fresh tears filled his eyes.

His hand was still trembling above the checkbook. "Would you really, Doctor Sondnes? Would you help us out like that?"

"Just don't go spreading it around town," she said as she walked over to the counter and started tapping at the keyboard. "I don't want everyone knowing that I'm bending the rules for -"

Before she could finish, she heard raised voices out in the waiting room. Turning to look at the door, she realized she could hear not only her nurse-slash-receptionist Rachel but also a worried-sounding female voice, accompanied by the sound of rushing footsteps. She knew something was wrong, but a moment later – before she had time to react – the door burst open and Rachel raced into the examination room with none of her usual calm and coolness.

"I'm sorry to interrupt," she said breathlessly, "but Lisa, we've got an emergency. Mrs. Dalton's dog Brian has been attacked by some kind of... monster!"

***

"Okay, just hold this here," Lisa said, grabbing Rachel's hand and forcing her to push down on the cotton bandage she'd placed on the dog's bleeding flank. "Don't let up, not even for a second, okay?"

"There's so much blood!" Rachel gasped.

"I know, he's lost a lot," Lisa replied, hurrying around to the other side of the table and grabbing a plastic box from the side. "Something's damn near ripped half his chest out."

"Is he going to make it?" Rachel asked.

"I don't know," Lisa said, taking out some medical strips and setting them down, then stepping over to the end of the table and reaching down to open Brian's eyes. A large and rather old fellow, Brian was breathing heavily but as she looked into his eyes Lisa at least saw some signs of life. "He's hanging on, but his vital signs are dropping," she continued, stepping back over to the middle of the table. "Keep holding that bandage down, Rachel, you're the only thing stopping him from bleeding out right now."

"What could have done this to him?" she asked.

"I have no idea," Lisa said as she grabbed a syringe and filled it from a small vial.

"Another dog?"

"Something bigger," Lisa continued. "Maybe. I'm not sure. There'll be time to figure that out later, but I've never seen damage quite like this. It's extreme, it's almost feral."

She stepped over to the end of the table again and injected Brian in the scruff of his neck. The fur was matted from a combination of blood and melted snow.

"This'll stop the pain," she told him. "You're going to drift off, Brian, and then... we're going to try to patch you up, okay? We're going to do everything we can to fix this, and with any luck you'll be right as rain soon."

"Should you be making promises like that?" Rachel asked.

Lisa looked over at her.

"You always told me," Rachel continued, "not to make unrealistic promises to people, in case we can't keep them. You said that's one of the most important rules."

"That's more about the owners," Lisa replied, hurrying around the table and looking down at the bandage, which was already filling up with more and more soaked blood. "When I ask you to move the bandage aside, I'm going to have to be really fast. He can't afford to lose much more blood or there'll be no getting him back. We don't have time to get all the usual equipment, he's deteriorating too fast, so we're going to have to do this the old-fashioned way." She glanced at the nurse. "My father taught me some of this stuff, but I never thought I'd have to actually use it. You might think I'm cutting corners here, Rachel, but I'm asking you to trust me because any other approach is going to fail Brian. Do you understand what I'm telling you?"

"Yes," Rachel replied, although her voice was faltering and she sounded increasingly unsure. "I mean... I think so. I mean... I'll do whatever you tell me to do, Doctor Sondnes. It's all for Brian, right?"

"It's all for Brian," Lisa said, taking a deep breath as she looked down at the blood-soaked bandage. "We're really not going to have long after the pressure's released. There's no room for error."

As she held the needle closed to the wound, she heard Brian's owner sobbing out in the waiting room. She swallowed hard, but she already knew that she was delaying the inevitable; the dog was on the brink of death already, and she was going to need a miracle if she had any hope of saving him at all.

"On my count," she continued. "Ready?"
"Ready."
"Three."
She moved the needle closer.
"Two."
"Come on, Brian," Rachel whispered. "You

can pull through."

"One!"

As soon as Rachel moved the bandage aside, more blood erupted from the central part of the wound. Lisa pushed her hands into the mess, trying to sew the edge section shut, but she quickly found that there was too much blood for her to even see what she was doing.

"Suction!" she yelled, and Rachel immediately introduced the suction extension to clear the site.

"I can barely tell where I am," Lisa muttered, already finding that so much of the flesh had been torn away, with thick strips hanging down and preventing her from finding a place to start with the needle. "What the hell happened here?"

"I've never seen anything like this," Rachel replied. "What did this to him?"

"Whatever it was," Lisa said, as more and more hot blood pumped out across her hands and she tried in vain to find a way to stem the flow, "it must have had teeth the size of my arm. I have no idea what was responsible for this mess, but I'm telling you one thing. In all my years and all my training, I've never seen anything that could have caused so much damage. At least, nothing that's supposed to live anywhere near Sobolton."

CHAPTER THREE

SNOW CONTINUED TO FALL so hard that the windscreen wipers could barely moved any out of the way at all, as John drove his cruiser slowly and carefully along the narrow and very icy forest road.

"Are you there yet?" Carolyn's voice asked, crackling over the radio. "I just spoke to Tommy and he's asking for you. He doesn't quite know what to do out there."

"Just give me a minute," John replied, glancing at the screen of his phone, which showed his progress along the road as well as a red marker at the edge of the lake. I'm still getting used to driving in this weather. These tires are helping a little, but not as much as I would've liked."

"Yeah, it's a nightmare out there," Carolyn

said. "It's always cold this time of year, but last night there was this real sudden snap that sent the temperature plunging. In all my years, that's a new one."

"I've never driven in such bad conditions before," he continued, squinting as he tried to spot the turn-off from the road. Seeing what *seemed* to be the right gap in the trees, he slowed the cruiser and prepared to turn the wheel, while preparing himself for the inevitable slide. "I don't get how you guys manage to shoot around when there's a blizzard coming down. It gets better in the summer, right?"

"Oh, totally," Carolyn replied, her voice momentarily becoming fuzzy and distorted over the radio. She added something else, something that John wasn't quite able to make out, before the reception cleared up just a little. "That's what they say, anyway. I was born in Sobolton so I don't really know what it's like to come here and have to get used to it. In some ways, this town is all I've ever known. Do you know what they say about local folk?"

"What do they say?" he asked, barely managing to focus on the conversation as he steered the cruiser onto what turned out to be a surprisingly steep road leading down toward the frozen lake.

"Enlighten me."

"They say we're born with skis on our feet," she told him.

"Sounds about right," he replied. "I'll have to give that a try. I've never been skiing but -"

Before he could finish, the cruiser lurched to one side. Although he tried to correct the slide by turning the wheel in the other direction, John was powerless to stop the vehicle bumping down the road, hitting numerous frozen ridges before spinning again until it began to reverse down toward the lake. For a few seconds John remained completely still, trying to work out what he should do next, before finally he took his foot off the throttle and pushed down slowly against the brake pedal, hoping to bring the vehicle to a halt. Glancing over his shoulder, he saw the frozen lake getting closer and closer; just as he began to worry that he might have to jump out of the cruiser, the right rear tire bumped at low speed against a frozen tree stump, spinning the vehicle slowly around and bringing it to a halt on an expanse of flat ground.

"What was that?" Carolyn asked. "Sorry, John, you broke up for a moment there."

"You have no idea," he murmured, still gripping the wheel for all he was worth, staring out at the huge pine trees rising up into the snowy sky.

A moment later he spotted several figures down by the lake about two hundred feet further alone the shore, and he realized that they were wearing the uniform of the Sobolton sheriff's department. "Okay," he added, "it's all good. I made it."

***

Still not feeling quite steady on his feet, and worried that he might slip at any moment, John crunched his way through the snow as he approached the half dozen officers who'd gathered not only on the snow but also out on the ice itself. Although his first thought was to order them back to the safety of the shore, as he looked out across the huge frozen lake John realized that these people were locals and that they probably knew best.

"I'm just a fish out of water," he said under his breath, before correcting himself. "Or a fish out of ice at this time of year."

Stopping, he saw that the men were gathered around one particular spot in the ice, and he realized that he could just about make out a dark shape beneath the surface. As one of the officers began to make his way over, John carefully eased himself down off the snowy bank and onto the ice, and he felt as if a thousand unused muscles in his legs were working overtime to keep him upright.

"You must be the new sheriff," the younger man said, walking across the ice with surprising ease, as if he was accustomed to such conditions. He held out a gloved hand. "Tommy Marshall. I'm your deputy."

"Nice to meet you," John said, reaching out to shake his hand, "I -"

Before he could finish, his right foot lost all grip, slipping wildly. Although he tried to catch the fall, John was powerless as his other foot slipped as well. His entire body felt as if it was rising up into the sky for a moment, then hovering in mid-air for an absurdly long period of time before he slammed down hard against the ice and let out a shocked gasp. He felt the ice's unforgiving strength holding firm against his body, as if all the shock-waves of the fall had been forced through his own muscles and bones, and for a few seconds he could only stare up at the gray sky and the drifting snow until finally the younger man's concerned face leaned into view.

"Sheriff?" Tommy said cautiously. "Are you..."

"I'm alright," John replied, slowly testing that statement by checking that he could move his fingers and toes. Once he was sure that he had no broken bones, he began to sit up, although he felt distinctly foolish for having fallen in the first place. "Just getting my... ice legs."

"Yeah, it can be tough," Tommy admitted, reaching out a hand and helping him up. "There's a saying about people like us who were born out here. Do you know what it is?"

"That you were born with skis on your feet?"

"Where did you hear that?" Tommy asked, clearly genuinely shocked.

"A little birdie told me," John replied, looking past him and seeing that the other officers were still gathered around the patch in the ice. "What have we got here?"

"Oh, right," Tommy said, taking him by the arm as if he was going to help him across the ice. "This way, and I'll show you."

"I think I'll be able to manage, thank you," John said, gently moving his hand away before gingerly stepping out toward the others. Immediately he almost slipped again; he managed to stay upright, although he could feel the muscles of his inner thighs working overtime and he knew that he probably looked distinctly foolish. "Just tell me what we're dealing with."

"Jerome Mackenzie called it in," Tommy

explained, walking alongside him as they approached the others. "He was out walking his dog Calvados and he spotted something. He thought it was nothing, but he came to get a closer look and... well, that's when he phoned me. We're on the same bowling team, you see, so he thought he'd give me a ring directly instead of going through the office, and I was nearby anyway so I came to take a look, and as soon as I saw it I called Carolyn. I knew today was your first day, I figured I'd be introduced to you properly later, but I suppose we're doing all of that now." He hesitated. "Aren't we?"

"What did this Jerome Mackenzie fellow actually find?" John asked, making his way painfully slowly toward the dark patch in the ice. "Sorry, I'm just... I'm really not used to this."

"You look like an infant learning to walk for the first time," Tommy told him.

John glanced at him.

"That was a bad attempt at humor," Tommy added, before gesturing toward the patch on the ice. "The temperature really dropped last night, just before two in the morning. We've had things like that before, but never so extreme. Despite the snow yesterday, the lake wasn't entirely frozen over until that plunge. I drove past myself yesterday evening and there were a few patches that were itching to get icy, but nothing like this. And then this morning the whole lake, from shore to shore, was frozen. Well, I suppose you can see that for yourself. Somehow the temperature really dropped through the floor. Anyway, and there's something frozen *in* it, trapped like... I don't know, like just frozen a few feet down there."

"A young girl?"

"Yeah," Tommy said, sounding a little nervous now. "Sir, I think you should prepare yourself. I don't know what your experience is like in law enforcement, but this really isn't a very pleasant sight."

"I wasn't expecting it to be," John said, finally reaching the other officers and looking round at them. "Good morning, gentlemen. My name's John Tench, you all know that and you know why I'm here, but we'll get to the formal introductions later. I look forward to getting to know each and every one of you." Looking down at the ice, he opened his mouth to say more, but at the last moment he was struck by the awful vision trapped a short distance between all their feet.

Reaching up, despite the snow, he instinctively removed his hat.

"What the hell?" he whispered, as the other men remained silent and the only sound came from more snow rustling as it landed all around them. "Who is she?"

CHAPTER FOUR

A KNOCK ON THE storeroom door finally shifted Lisa from her daze. Sitting on one of the plastic chairs, her shirt drenched in blood and with more blood smeared all across her hands and arms and face, she turned and looked across the storeroom just as the door inched open.

"Hey," Rachel said softly, her voice punctuating the silence. "How are you doing in here?"

"Just... cleaning up," Lisa said, although she knew that explanation made no sense since she was still filthy, and especially because there was no sink in the storeroom. "I just... needed a moment."

"I get it," Rachel continued, keeping her voice low, "it's just that Mrs. Dalton has been asking questions, and I've done my best to answer them but I don't think she wants to talk to the monkey. I think she wants to talk to the organ grinder." She paused. "Sorry if that's not quite the appropriate phrase to use in this situation."

"No, it's fine," Lisa replied wearily, getting to her feet. "Give me a minute or two to *actually* clean myself up and then I'll come through and talk to her. Have you filled her in on the basics?"

Rachel nodded.

"Thanks," Lisa said, glancing briefly at an electrical socket on the wall before turning to Rachel again. "Honestly, I'll be right through." She held up her hands to reveal all the blood smeared down to her elbows. "I really think I should get clean first. Just give me a moment to get all this blood off."

***

"Somehow," she said a few minutes later, standing at the desk in the reception area in a fresh shirt that she always brought to work in case of emergencies, "we managed to stop the bleeding, so at the moment Brian's in what we call a serious but stable condition."

"But he's alive?" Rosemary Dalton replied, her eyes still filled with tears. "Please, tell me that he's alive!"

"Yeah, he is," Lisa said, "but he lost a lot of

blood and he's not out of the woods yet."

"I was so sure you wouldn't be able to save him," Rosemary continued, using the side of her hand to wipe away some of the tears. "I was sitting in here and I could hear you shouting at each other in the surgery room, and I just had this really strong feeling that it wasn't going to work. I was scared that by trying, we were just torturing him."

"He's a strong boy," Lisa told her. "Not many dogs would have got this far."

"My insurance -"

"Rachel will talk to you about that," Lisa said, interrupting her, "but we'll figure something out."

"I don't know what happened," Rosemary said. "We were out walking, we were in the forest but not far, I could still see our back door. We live over on Bodaro Road, and I always take Brian out early so he can run off some energy before breakfast. He goes off the leash, but never far. He's a good boy."

"Did you see what attacked him?"

"He went over the ridge," Rosemary continued. "Just for a second. He'd been out of my sight barely long enough for me to blink, and I wasn't worried at all, but then I heard him let out this furious bark like nothing I've ever heard from him before. It was like..."

She paused for a few seconds, staring into

space as if she was trying to remember exactly what had happened. And then:

"Arrrooooooorrrr!" she screamed suddenly, shocking both Lisa and Rachel.

After that, silence returned to the reception room. Looking over at the bench opposite, Lisa saw a bloodied coat that had been laid out. Evidently this coat had been wrapped around the injured dog and used to keep him warm while he was transported to the office.

"And then," Rosemary continued, "his bark was cut off really suddenly, like choked off, by the most dreadful cry of pain. Agony, really. Just the sound of a body suffering something awful, and that was like..."

She paused again.

Lisa tilted her head.

"Gaaaaarrrhhhhhhh!" Rosemary screamed, gripping the side of the desk. "Grooowwaaaaahlll!"

Rachel looked at Lisa, who was focused very much on Rosemary's pale features.

"It went down at the end slightly," Rosemary said, "like I tried to mimic just then. Did you hear that?"

"I think so," Lisa replied.

"I was so terrified," Rosemary explained. "I just knew right away that something was awfully wrong, that the cries of pain I heard came from my boy. I stood there frozen staring up at that ridge, wondering what could possibly be going on up there, and after a few more seconds I realized that I could hear a struggle. Brian was growling and trying to scare off his attacker, and something else was growling as well, something that sounded nothing like a dog."

She paused.

Lisa opened her mouth to ask whether -

"Graggggg!" Rosemary snarled throatily, her voice filled with a kind of bloody animal anger that seemed almost impossible given her demure appearance. "Gzzzrgl!"

She took a deep breath, as if she needed to take a few seconds to compose herself.

"Like that," she added. "I've got a lot of experience with dogs, and I'm telling you, it was no dog. And then Brian came back into view, dragging himself over the top of the ridge and then tumbling down, leaving this trail of blood in the snow. He landed right at my feet, and I saw that my poor baby darling was bleeding heavily on his side. He'd obviously put up a hell of a fight, he'd never back down, not against anything. I got down on my knees, I thought he was dead right then and there, but he was panting hard and I realized after a moment what he was doing." She clenched both fists and held them up high. "He was still fighting! Whatever had happened to him, he was saying no, he was saying this isn't happening today! He was saying that he refused to die like that!"

"He's a fighter, alright," Lisa acknowledged.

"I took off my coat," Rosemary continued, "and I bundled him up in it. I picked him up and I turned away to carry him to the car so I could bring him here, but then at the last second..."

Her voice trailed off, and once again she appeared to be reliving the entire awful experience in her mind.

"I saw it," she added, as fresh tears began to fill her eyes. "I saw the beast, the monster that had done this to my poor baby. It was at the top of the ridge, staring down at us both, almost as if it was celebrating its victory, as if it was proud of what it had done. It was a wolf, Doctor Sondnes, or at least that's how it presented itself, but I've seen wolves and this wolf was not quite... right."

"In what way?" Lisa asked.

"It was big," Rosemary explained, "and strong, and it had my Brian's blood all around its muzzle. But what struck me the most about this monstrosity of nature was the way it looked at me. This thing didn't display one ounce of fear, or shame, or regret. It had emerged from the forest and it had come to the very point where the forest bleeds into the world of man, to the ecotone where by right any living creature should show some caution, but there was none of that. All creatures belong to one world or another, Doctor Sondnes. They might tread in other worlds from time to time, but they *belong* only in one. That's as true of humans as it is of any animal."

Rachel opened her mouth to reply, before turning to Lisa, who in turn kept her gaze fixed firmly on Rosemary.

"But this thing," the older woman continued, "did not belong only to one world or the other. It belonged to both, and it was so proud of that fact. So proud, indeed, that it was standing there defiantly as if to prove it, as if to say it wanted me to look at it and to understand it and to fear it. And then, as I stood there holding my whimpering Brian in my arms, with his blood soaking through the fabric of my best coat, the beast that attacked him turned around and trudged away into the forest as if nothing had happened, as if it had done what it came to do and now it was going away for a while. I could feel the arrogance radiating from its soul. Yet somehow, in the way it walked or in some other manner that I don't quite understand, I could sense the true message of its appearance, which was that... it would be back."

She fell silent, as if in awe of what she'd just said.

"Well," Lisa replied finally, before taking a moment to clear her throat, "we don't usually get wolves in this part of the county. There was a new mandate passed last year, though, so if there *has* been a wolf sighting then I'm obliged to report it to the sheriff's department."

CHAPTER FIVE

THEY STOOD IN A circle on the ice, each man looking down at the girl who lay frozen a couple of feet beneath the surface of the frozen lake.

She was young, they could all see that, perhaps only eight or nine years old. Her pale face stared back up at them, her eyes frozen open and her hair held out mid-flow in strands amid the ice. She was almost in a star position, her arms and legs reaching away from her body, which in turn was clothed in a black dress with patterns of white and red. No shoes covered her feet, which instead were bare; bloodied marks could be seen on the skin of her hands and face, and scratches criss-crossed her feet and ankles, and a couple of heavy bruises had started to develop on one side of her jaw and cheek before freezing with the rest of her. And all around, frozen into the ice just as she herself was frozen, whispers of curled blood hung as if they'd been in the process of leaking out and away from her body. Between her and the men observing her, certain irregularities and imperfections in the ice crafted small distortions.

Snow was still falling, perhaps a little heavier than before.

"Who is she?" John asked finally, before looking around at the officers. "Does anyone know?"

He waited; most of the men remained silent, while a couple solemnly shook their heads.

"Well, she's a child," John continued, trying not to sound frustrated as he looked back down at the dead girl. "Someone has to know who she is. Someone has to be missing her."

"I checked about twenty minutes ago," Tommy said gingerly. "No children have been reported missing in the area over the past few days."

"Well, one must have been," John replied, "or if not, then she's from further away, or for some reason someone hasn't wanted to report that she's gone. There has to be someone out there somewhere who knows who she is." He paused, looking down once more at the girl's frozen dead eyes. "She has to have a name. And a home."

"There might be some clues on her," Tommy pointed out. "Something in her pockets, or in her dress, or she might even have some kind of medical records we can access. There was a case once where a body was found burned about twenty miles from here in the forest, we didn't have much to go on but the deceased had undergone hip surgery a few years earlier. We were able to identify them by running the serial number on their implant." He paused. "In theory, the same thing might work again if this girl had something like that. Of course, the situation's pretty different. That guy was burned. This girl is frozen."

"Doesn't look like that's what killed her, though," one of the other officers murmured.

"No, it doesn't," John agreed. "I'm seeing cuts and bruises and other signs of trauma. Is it possible she was dumped here right before the lake froze?" He waited for an answer, before looking around at the rest of them. "I don't know the climate here too well. Would the lake freeze that fast?"

"It's possible," Tommy admitted. "A little unlikely, sure, but... possible."

"In all likelihood," John continued, "someone out there is frantically searching for this child. I'd be very surprised if, by the end of the day, we don't hear about a missing little girl who matches this description. By then I'd like to have some idea of what we can tell people."

"Agreed," Tommy said, before pausing for a few seconds. "But... Sir, I mean... she's trapped in the ice. So how do we get to her?"

***

The bands and metal teeth of the chainsaw rattled slightly as they moved through the snowy air. Not yet switched on, the chainsaw still made for a formidable sight as it swung, held tight in the slightly dirty gloved hand of the man who – just moments earlier – had hauled it out of his truck before setting out across the ice.

"Walt Jordan," Tommy said, stepping forward and reaching out to shake the man's one free hand. "Good to see you, Walt. Thanks for coming out under these circumstances. Allow me to introduce you to John Tench, the new sheriff of Sobolton."

His face mostly hidden beneath a huge beard, an equally huge mustache and an even bigger pair of eyebrows, set beneath a peaked orange cap, Walt turned and looked at John. Pausing for a moment, as if not quite sure what to make of this new arrival, Walt hesitated before finally reaching out and shaking the man's hand with a grunt.

"Hello, Mr. Jordan," John said, "I'm told you've got a lot of land to the north of town. I bet there's some prime fishing to be done up there."

Walt grunted again as he pulled his hand away.

"Walt runs a kind of ecological paradise," Tommy explained somewhat cautiously. "He's trying to put as much into his land while taking as little as possible out. He's actually a committed vegan, he invests in all this new technology that he thinks the rest of us'll end up using a few years from now. I went out there once and got a look at some bits of it, and I thought it was impressive. Some of it. Some of it I didn't quite understand, but I could kinda tell that it's smart. It went right over my head, that's for sure."

"Huh," John said, looking Walt up and down, noting the man's dirty orange overalls. "Well, Mr. Jordan, I'm not a vegan myself, but I can certainly respect anyone who tries to have a positive impact on the environment around him. I'd still love to see what kind of operation you're running up there, it sounds fascinating."

Walt simply stared at him for a moment, before managing another grunt. Already, fresh falling snow was starting to land on his immense facial hair, although any on the center of his mustache quickly melted in the heat emanating from two cavernous and rather busy nostrils.

"You're probably wondering why we called you out here," John said, turning and gesturing toward the dark patch in the lake. "I'm afraid it's a sensitive and rather unpleasant situation, and I'm truly sorry that you have to see this. To be honest, I assumed we'd have some other way of getting through the ice, but I'm informed that this is by far the quickest method and that you're the right man for the job." He glanced briefly at Tommy. "I guess people do things differently out here. I respect that."

Tommy offered an apologetic shrug.

"There's a deceased young girl trapped in the lake," John continued, as Walt stepped past him and then stopped to look down at the corpse. "As you can see, she's aged somewhere between... I'd say eight and ten. Until we get her out and defrost her... I'm not sure that's quite the word I should have used, but I hope you understand what I mean. We need to extract her from the ice without disturbing the scene, and while I have my reservations about this approach, my deputy here informs me that you know a way of cutting through and assisting us." Sighing, he realized that he perhaps wasn't quite explaining himself properly, although that was mainly due to the fact that he wasn't quite convinced by the approach they were taking. "I'll keep this short and simple, Mr. Jordan. Can you get the girl out of the ice for us?"

Walt stared down at the body for a few seconds.

"I'm *really* not sure if this is the best approach," John said, turning to Tommy. "There has to be a better way to get the body out. Why don't we take a few minutes to search online and find out which agency would be most appropriate for -"

Before he could finish, the chainsaw revved to life, drowning out any hope of conversation. Startled, John and the others stepped back closer to the shoreline, watching as Walt moved the chainsaw's tip down to the ice. As soon as contact was made, an ear-piercing grinding sound rang out, filling the air as the chainsaw's teeth tried to cut furiously beneath the surface. John instinctively looked at his feet for a moment, worried that cracks might appear at any moment to portend the entire frozen lake breaking up, but to his immense relief he saw no such thing. Instead, he looked over at Walt again, and he could only watch for the next couple of minutes as the huge man tried and failed to cut through the icy surface. At least, he noticed, the man using the chainsaw had what appeared to be another set of chains wrapped around his shoes to provide extra grip.

Finally Walt stepped back and switched the chainsaw off, before turning to the gathered officers and letting out yet another grunt.

"It's no good," Tommy said, seemingly interpreting for the fellow as he turned to John. "The ice is just too... icy, I suppose. I don't think he thinks there's any point carrying on. And to be honest, when it comes to cutting things and breaking through things, Walt tends to be the expert around here."

"Okay, I think I might actually be slightly relieved that we're not going to start carving the crime scene up," John said, looking at the ice and seeing that the surface had barely even been scratched. "But in that case, we need to find some other way to get that poor girl out. We sure can't leave her down there."

CHAPTER SIX

"YES, BUT, I'D LIKE to see the sheriff, please," Lisa said, standing in the reception area while also listening to another voice on her cellphone. "No, sorry, I wasn't talking to you," she continued, "I was talking to the..."

She sighed.

"Hold on, please."

Lowering the phone, she stepped over to the desk and set a simple folder down.

"Hey," she continued, "Carolyn, this is important, I need to see -"

"And I told you," Carolyn replied, glaring up at her, "he's not available right now."

"When *will* he be available?"

"For operational reasons," Carolyn said dourly, "I'm not able to give out details on investigations that this office might or might not be running. In addition, for reasons of security, I can't give out details on the location of staff-members who -"

"Okay, fine," Lisa sighed, "I get it."

"Terrorist threats -"

"I'm not a terrorist, Carolyn," Lisa said pointedly, "I'm the local veterinarian. And I had a situation this morning that I'm mandated to report." She paused for a moment. "Listen, fine, whatever. I don't suppose I need to see him face-to-face, but can you please make sure that he takes a look at this letter? I just have to let him know that there's been a report of a wolf attack in the area, and he should probably consider sending a patrol out to check for activity. This particular attack was very close to housing, so I'm concerned that the wolf in question might be dangerous. It might also be unusually bold, and willing to approach human habitation."

"Did it attack a person?" Carolyn asked, sounding a little nervous now.

"No, it did not," Lisa explained. "It attacked a dog, and that dog is currently fighting for his life at my surgery. But I can't guarantee that a human won't be next, especially if – as I suspect – this wolf is particularly hungry. I know this might not seem very important, Carolyn, and I know you and I aren't particularly great buddies, but I really need you to make sure that the new sheriff gets my report. It's got my contact details at the top, including my email address, so would you please ask him to get in touch?"

"I'll do my best," Carolyn replied, setting the file on top of a small pile of papers at the edge of the desk. "Will there be anything else, Ms. Sondnes?"

"No," Lisa said, turning and heading to the door, before glancing back at her. "Oh, and as you already know, Carolyn... it's *Doctor* Sondnes."

With that she headed outside, leaving Carolyn to roll her eyes and – once she was sure she couldn't be seen – raise her right hand and extend the middle digit.

***

"I'm sorry about that," Lisa said as she made her way across the parking lot at the front of the station, taking her keys from her pocket. "I've been trying to juggle about a million things at once all morning, and this snow really isn't helping. How are things going for you down there?"

"Not great," Wade replied, his voice sounding patchy over the phone. "This storm is backing us up, and I think I'm gonna be a few more days." He paused for a few seconds. "I miss you."

"I miss you too," Lisa said, stopping next to her car and looking along the street. She saw the lights of a local bar in the distance, and for a few seconds she wondered whether she could perhaps drop by for a quick lunchtime pick-me-up. "I really wish you were here right now."

"Me too," he told her, "but work's work."

"I know."

"And it's a big job," he continued with a heavy sigh that was even audible over the crackling line. "They want us to install all these pipes, but they ordered the wrong connectors and now we've got to try to make them fit anyway, because they don't have the budget to fix it properly. You know when people wonder why stuff breaks all the time? It's because people like me weren't given the tools to do the job properly in the first place."

"Couldn't you complain or something?" she asked, brushing snow from her hair as she continued to watch the bar.

"They'd fire me and get someone else in," he countered. "It's not like it's dangerous, no-one's gonna get hurt because of this. It'll just break five times faster than it should, and then some corporation'll demand loads of taxpayer money to sort it out, and a load of executives'll farm out the job to the lowest bidder while pocketing the difference as part of their bonuses. I'm sorry, do I sound cynical?"

"Only a little bit," she told him, "and that's why I -"

Stopping herself just in time, she realized that she'd almost dropped the l-bomb, even though she and Wade weren't quite at that level yet. She felt they *should* be, since they'd been dating for a year and living together for a few months, but somehow neither of them had quite got to that point; hugely relieved that she hadn't blurted something so important out in such a trivial setting, she realized after a few seconds that she was still staring at the distant bar at the other end of the snowstorm-ravaged main street. Somehow the neon lights above the entrance seemed almost to be calling to her.

"I'd better let you get back to work," she said after a moment. "The sooner you finish, the sooner you can get back to Sobolton. Provided all the roads aren't closed, at least."

"Which they probably will be right now," he pointed out. "Listen, I miss you and I -"

He fell silent for a moment.

"I promise I'll be home by Sunday," he added, sounding a little awkward. "If I have to trek through the snow myself, then that's what I'll do, because I've already been away for too long. I don't mind spending so much time with the guys, you know that, but there comes a time when I want a woman's touch. I can't wait to get home, Lisa, and crawl into bed and remind you just how crazy you make me. I hope you haven't forgotten that already."

"Nope," she said, forcing a smile. "Hey, listen, I'm going to go. Speak soon, okay?"

Once she'd cut the call, she found herself still standing next to the car, still watching the bar. She tried to remind herself how good she'd feel if she simply headed back to the office without having a drink first, but at the same time she knew that she only had to get on with some paperwork, so it wasn't as if she needed to be absolutely at the top of her game. Sure, an emergency case might be rushed in, but she'd already dealt with one emergency that day and she knew from experience that there were never two during the same shift. The bar was waiting there for her, and more than anything she wanted to squirrel herself away in one of the corner booths and just get some time to herself, away from all the drama and trouble of the town.

Finally, feeling herself weaken and promising that she'd only have one drink, she slipped her keys away before stepping past the car and onto the snowy sidewalk.

"Hey!" a voice called out.

Startled, Lisa turned to see Annie Dennis making her way over, dressed from head-to-toe in thick winter clothing.

"Stranger, how are you doing?" Annie laughed, grabbing Lisa's arm and then giving her a big hug. "I feel like I haven't seen you in forever! How's life going as Sobolton's only veterinarian?"

"Good," Lisa replied, feeling as if she'd just been shaken out of a dream, and intensely relieved that she hadn't actually managed to get all the way over to the bar. "Yeah, I'm just... getting on with things and trying to keep out of trouble."

"Aren't we all?" Annie said, stepping back from the hug. "Hey, this might seem like a crazy idea, but I just finished all my errands for the day and I've got the entire afternoon off! How about a cheeky little drink down the road, for old times' sake? You and I have so much to catch up on!"

"We do," Lisa said cautiously, her mind racing as she tried to think of an excuse. She glanced at the bar again, and then she pulled her keys back out of her pocket, "and I'd love to get a drink some other time. It's just that I'm snowed under right now, no pun intended, and I need to get back to the office. I only popped over here to drop in a report at the sheriff's office about a wolf that was seen in the area."

"A wolf?" Annie replied, her eyes opening wide with shock. "That doesn't sound good. Should we be worried?"

"I'm sure the new sheriff will have it all under control," Lisa told her, before heading back to her car and opening the door. "Don't worry, Annie. Everything's going to be absolutely fine!"

AMY CROSS

CHAPTER SEVEN

SNOW WAS FALLING HARDER now, blown through the air by a quickening wind, as John stood on the ice and stared down at the frozen girl beneath his feet. He could see a few bare scratches in the ice's surface, marks showing where Walt's chainsaw had failed; the marks criss-crossed above the girl's frozen face.

"So," Tommy said, making his way back over from the shoreline, where the other deputies had gathered to discuss the matter, "we've been talking and one of the guys came up with a good point."

"What's the good point?" John asked, not taking his gaze off the dead girl.

"Well, Ronnie pointed out that although she sure *looks* real, we don't know that she's real."

John turned to him.

"She might be a doll," Tommy continued nervously. "She might just be a really... really lifelike doll, maybe one that someone put there as a prank. And then they're filming us from a distance, having a great laugh at our expense." He looked toward the trees on the far side of the lake. "They might be tiktokking us or whatever it's called right now."

"There's blood in the water," John said, somewhat bemused by Tommy's suggestion.

"That might be fake too."

"I don't think this is fake," John told him.

"Well, I made a call to see what can be done," Tommy continued, "and apparently there's some industrial-grade equipment that they can use to get her out, but because of the storm and the conditions, and the late notice and the fact that it's already getting close to midday, not to mention -"

"Cut to the chase," John said, interrupting him. "Please."

"Well, it can't be here until tomorrow morning."

"Tomorrow morning?"

Tommy nodded.

"That's quite a fair way off," John pointed out.

"So what we could do," Tommy continued, "is put out some markers just to kind of warn people away until the equipment gets here."

"What do you mean?" John asked.

"So that people don't come and look at her," Tommy said, although the caution in his voice suggested that – at least on some deep level – he knew this idea wasn't going to fly. "We wouldn't want people coming and taking photos of her, would we?"

"We would not," John agreed.

"I don't see what else we can do," Tommy told him. "We can't get her out, so we can't move her. And this storm's not going anywhere for at least the rest of the day, and it's not like we can just stand around here guarding her." He waited for a response, but John's stare was starting to make him feel uncomfortable. "Can we?"

"I want one man here at all times," John said firmly. "She's not being left alone."

"Is that strictly necessary?"

"It's the right thing to do," John countered.

"Right."

"I know it's cold and inhospitable, and not the best job in the world," John continued, "but sometimes police work's like that." He looked at the other men, who were still huddled on the shore. "Just arrange short shifts," he added, "and maybe have them work in pairs instead of alone. They can sit in their vehicles if that helps, they shouldn't freeze. And have them check in every two hours, just so we know that they're on the ball. Not only is it the right thing to do by this poor girl, it's also the only way we can be sure the crime scene isn't disturbed."

"Right," Tommy said again, sounding even less certain now. "And is that... all day?"

"All day."

"But not at night," Tommy said. "It's going to get real cold out here overnight."

John let out a sigh.

"Well," Tommy added, "I -"

"I'll do the night shift," John told him, struggling to hide a sense of extreme irritation. "I'll do the whole damn night shift on my own, from sundown to sunrise." He paused for a moment, hoping that he'd made his point. "And I won't complain about it, either," he added finally. "Now let's get organized so that everyone knows exactly what they're doing. Then I'm heading back into town to finish up a few things at the office before coming out here again tonight." He looked down at the girl beneath the ice again. "She's not going to be left alone. Not for a second. We're going to do the right thing here."

"Sure," Tommy said. "Absolutely. That's what I would have decided to."

"And I'm going to need some help getting my cruiser back up to the road," John said firmly. "Any volunteers?"

***

"She might be a doll," John muttered sarcastically under his breath as he drove carefully along the icy road leading back into town. "Someone might just be pulling some elaborate practical joke on us for reasons that defy all logic."

He slowed the cruiser as he navigated a tight right-hand turn. Ahead, he could see the lights of Sobolton just about managing to shine through the winter squall.

"Or she might actually be a real girl, but let's just leave her out there until we can get her out of the ice." He gripped the steering wheel a little tighter. "Who cares if she's all alone? Who cares if it's disrespectful? Who cares if -"

Suddenly something darted out from the trees, racing straight in front of the cruiser. John immediately slammed his foot on the brake pedal, bringing the cruiser to an abrupt halt – albeit one with a slight slide. Once the vehicle was stopped, he sat in silence for a moment with the windshield wipers still running; he was still very much unfamiliar with driving in such bad conditions, but he couldn't help thinking that he'd felt a faint bump as he'd come to a halt. He looked straight ahead, watching for any further sign of the creature, but he was fairly sure that nothing had run off past the other side of the road.

Finally, unbuckling his seat-belt, John opened the door and stepped out into the snow. He reached for his gun, but only to check that it was secure; he left it in its holster as, a few seconds later, he heard a faint snarling sound coming from somewhere around the front of the vehicle.

Stepping around past the door, he walked to the front and looked down. To his immense relief, he saw no sign of any kind of injured animal, although after a moment he spotted a few dark dots in the snow. Crouching down, he peered at the dots and realized that they might be blood. He looked around again; the road stretched away into the distance, curving down the hill toward Sobolton, but the only movement came from the relentlessly falling snow that seemed somehow to be getting even heavier as the day progressed.

A moment later, hearing another snarling sound, John looked at the front of the cruiser, and then he realized that whatever he'd hit seemed to have crawled beneath the vehicle.

"Hell," he whispered, getting to his feet and stepping back, then crouching down and trying to get a view between the wheels. "What the hell *is* this thing?"

As he squinted slightly, he realized that he could just about make out a shape, a dark mass, shaking violently beneath the cruiser. The animal –

whatever it might be – had evidently been hurt and was now seeking refuge; whatever it was, John could tell that it was big, and after a few more seconds he realized that he could hear a faint whimper mixed in with a low, recurring growl.

"Damn it," he muttered, getting to his feet. "You're not gonna want to just come out of there easily, are you? And I don't fancy trying to drag you out. So what are we going to do here?"

Heading back to the side of the cruiser, he climbed back into the driver's seat and reached for the radio.

"Hey, Carolyn," he said, "what -"

Before he could finish, he heard a loud thud coming from somewhere beneath the vehicle, and his entire seat shook briefly. He looked down just in time to hear another thud, then a third, and then he leaned over and saw to his surprise that something had punctured the bottom of the cruiser, ripping the metal. A moment later he heard a snarling sound nearby, and he turned just in time to see a dark shape rushing unsteadily into the darkness of the forest on the other side of the road.

"Hey!" he shouted, although he knew he was already too late.

Climbing back out of the cruiser, he walked over to the side of the road and looked between the trees. He instinctively reached for his gun, just in case it might be needed; when he glanced down at the snow on the ground, he saw more spots of blood. Whatever he'd hit, the creature was clearly injured, although it had still manage to move with a fine turn of speed.

"Sheriff?" Carolyn's voice said, crackling slightly over the radio in the cruiser. "Are you there? What's up?"

CHAPTER EIGHT

"OKAY, BRIAN," LISA SAID, as she peered at the stitches on the dog's flank, "these are looking pretty good so far. Let's just keep doing what we're doing, and cross our fingers."

She looked at the side of the dog's head. Heavily sedated, Brian was breathing slowly but steadily, and he was showing remarkable resilience. He wasn't out of the woods yet, of course, but he was through the most dangerous phase and for the first time Lisa was actually starting to feel a slowly-growing sense of hope.

"How's he doing?" Rachel whispered, leaning into the room from the brightly-lit corridor.

"Better than I expected," Lisa replied, heading over to join her. "I'll give Rosemary a call a little later, just before we shut. The poor woman must be worried sick."

"As long as she doesn't start doing animal impressions again."

Stepping out into the corridor, Lisa gently bumped the door shut. She had a million items of paperwork that needed filing, but for a moment she stood lost in thought, thinking back to the initial sight of Brian as he'd been carried bleeding into the surgery. She'd seen some terrible injuries over the years, but something about this particular case had left her feeling a little shaken, as if she couldn't quite get her head around what had happened. She liked knowing, and in that moment she felt there was a lot she still didn't understand.

"Do you think something's out there?" Rachel asked suddenly.

"What?"

"Something dangerous," Rachel continued. "I don't even know what I mean, to be honest. I just hate the idea that something came out of the forest and attacked that poor dog, and then it just retreated and now no-one know where it is or what even *what* it is. It's not as if it's going to just attack once and then go away, is it? And Brian's a big dog, so obviously this thing isn't exactly scared of a fight." She paused for a moment, clearly close to tears. "Lisa, I know I'm probably overreacting, but isn't there a danger that this thing could attack humans? Are our children safe?"

"I've left a report for the new sheriff," Lisa replied, "and I'm hoping he'll call me back pretty soon."

"I haven't really heard anything about the guy. Do you think he'll do anything?"

"I don't know," Lisa said, before pausing for a moment. "To be honest, if I were you, I wouldn't hold my breath. This kind of thing isn't exactly going to be a priority unless someone photogenic gets hurt." She looked along the corridor for a moment, already wondering whether she could perhaps sneak away from work early and hit the bar for one quick drink; after a few seconds, however, she realized that a better bet would be to find some kind of distraction. "That's why," she added, "we sometimes have to take matters into our own hands."

***

"Come on, Dad," she muttered about one hour later, as she opened the rickety old box in the garage at home. "Let's see what you left in here."

As a couple of spiders scurried away into the corners, startled after two years of peace, Lisa reached past the cobwebs and began to lift the old rifle off its hook. She'd been meaning to check her father's little stash for a while, ever since his death a few summers earlier, but somehow she'd always managed to put the moment off. Now, as she stepped back and brushed some more cobwebs from the rifle, she allowed herself a faint involuntary smile as she remembered her father holding the weapon. His hands had been so much bigger; now, in her own hands, Lisa felt as if it was the rifle itself that appeared to have grown.

"Now you hold this," she remembered Rod's voice saying, as he'd taken her hands and forced them into the right position. "Just like that. Does it feel natural?"

"I think so," she'd replied, although as a little girl she'd never been too interested in hunting. She'd always preferred the idea of saving animals, and back then she'd believed the world was black and white. "It's heavy."

"Wait 'til it's loaded," her father had chuckled. "Now, you might not immediately like this thing, Lisa, but we live in a place where it's kinda necessary to know how to handle yourself. You don't want to be reliant on other people, do you?"

Now, standing in the garage with a decades-old conversation ringing in her ears, Lisa checked the tip of the gun and took a few seconds to blow away more cobwebs.

"Today I'm going to show you how to clean a gun," she heard her father saying, from a different conversation altogether. "Pay attention, because one day this might save your life."

"Dad, can I go inside?" she remembered whingeing. "I'm really not into this."

"It's not a matter of being into it," he'd insisted. "It won't take long, and your little television shows can wait."

At the time she'd pretended to pay attention, but in truth she had no real idea how to clean the rifle. She checked that it wasn't loaded, a task that was easy yet one she still found satisfying. Brief flashes of the process were floating in her mind, although she supposed that she could possibly do some quick research online; at the same time, the rifle seemed to be in pretty good condition, and as she raised it and turned, aiming at the far end of the gloomy garage, she already felt as if she was taking too many precautions. She pretended to aim at one of the boxes set against the far wall, and then she pulled the trigger, resulting in nothing more than a harmless clicking sound.

"It's not like I'm really going to need it," she said to herself, before setting the rifle down and then turning to one of the other cabinets.

Crouching down, she pulled the cabinet's door open and saw lots of old-fashioned cardboard boxes arranged all higgledy-piggledy, some on their sides and some having partially fallen open. Almost every box bore a different brand logo, and as she pulled a few out Lisa wondered just how her father had acquired such a myriad assortment of ammunition over the years. She opened the first box and saw some cartridges inside but even with her lack of expert knowledge she knew these were for a different gun.

"Great," she muttered, "it's going to be like some kind of puzzle."

She opened another box, then another, before finally finding one that might be useful. Taking out one of the long bullets, she turned it around between her fingers and then she tried to load it into the rifle. To her surprise, the bullet was a perfect fit, so she reached into the box and took out a handful more. As she did so, she looked at the box and made a mental note of the various numbers on the side, although she hesitated as she saw that these particular bullets were supposedly tipped with silver.

Picking up one bullet to check, she saw that the very top was indeed colored different to the main body.

"Huh," she said, before adding this bullet to the collection of around a dozen in her pocket. "Dad, you were crazy, she said with a smile. "I love you, but you were completely nuts."

***

Slamming her car door shut, Lisa took a moment to

adjust her jacket. Snow was still falling hard and fast, and she was starting to wonder whether she might be making a mistake; at the same time, with her father's old rifle slung over her shoulder, she reminded herself that she wasn't exactly planning on setting out for a long hike.

She'd parked by the side of the road, a little way from Rosemary Dalton's house. A steep snowbank rose up from the road's opposite side, reaching to the edge of the forest. This was around a quarter of a mile from the spot where Brian had been attacked, and Lisa figured that if there was any wolf activity in the area, she should be able to find it pretty quickly. She wasn't even convinced yet that Brian's attacker *had* been a wolf, but she wanted to know for certain and she also wanted to be able to present the new sheriff with actual documented facts rather than speculation.

Besides, she knew she was safe. She knew how to at least handle a gun.

"Hold it up like this," she remembered her father explaining on one of their hunting trips, when he'd tried to get her more interested in his hobby. "You'll get used to the weight. Try to focus on aiming straight."

"If you could see me now," she said under her breath, before stepping out across the icy road, quickly reaching the snowbank and picking a shallower section that might make climbing a little easier. "I'm not quite such a pen-pusher after all, huh?"

Reaching the top of the snowbank on all fours, she stumbled to her feet and looked ahead into the forest. The ground rose gently between the thin, dark trees, and the afternoon light had already begun to dull a little. Once again, Lisa was briefly filled with the sense that she was being a fool, but she knew the alternative would be to sit around drinking, and instead she wanted to be proactive. Besides, there was almost certainly no danger, and she knew she could protect herself if necessary.

She set out through the snow, which turned out to be a little deeper than she'd imagined. By the time she'd passed three trees her knees were already aching, but she had no intention of turning back now. As she reached out and steadied herself against one of the trees, she heard the howl of wind ripping its way through the forest, almost crying out as it raced down from the gray sky.

CHAPTER NINE

"YOU SHOULD HAVE SEEN it," Joe Hicks said as he sat on a stool in McGinty's. "I'm telling you, a man always remembers a fish like that. There are half a dozen throughout my whole life that I'll never forget."

"You'll have time to catch some more now," Pete said, drying some glasses on the other side of the bar. "Got a life of luxury ahead of you."

"As if," Joe snorted. "Meryl's never gonna stop finding little jobs for me to do around the house now that I'm officially retired. She's already acting as if I'm taking up a new job as her personal dogsbody."

Hearing the door swing open, he turned to see John Tench stepping into the bar. The young man immediately removed his hat before gently pushing the door shut.

"And here comes my replacement," Joe said with a faint, amused smile. "Mr. Tench, I have to admit that I didn't think you were the kind of man to pop into a place like this at lunchtime. Not that I'm criticizing. Just observing."

"Afternoon, Joe," John said as he wandered over to join him at the bar. "I just got back to the station and Carolyn told me I might find you here."

"Can I get you a beer?" Pete asked. "On the house, as a welcome gift."

"Not right now, thanks," John replied, sitting on the stool next to Joe. "I've got to admit, I've already had quite the morning. Did you hear about the body we found out at the lake?"

"I did, as it happens," Joe told him. "I suppose in some way this is Sobolton welcoming you and letting you know that things aren't gonna be easy." He paused for a moment. "Carolyn told me it's a young girl."

John nodded, before glancing around.

"If you're thinking of keeping it a secret," Joe continued, "then think again. People talk round these parts, John. If I hadn't mentioned it, they'd have heard about it all from someone else soon enough."

Making brief eye contact with several of the bar's patrons, John quickly realized that Joe was probably right; keeping secrets seemed difficult in

Sobolton.

"This is a part of the job that I'm definitely not gonna miss," Joe continued. "Have you identified her yet?"

"She's still in the ice," John explained. "We got a guy named Walt out to try to cut her free, but he barely made a dent."

"Walt's one of the good ones around here," Joe told him.

"Now we've got to wait until tomorrow," John continued, still wary of revealing too much in public. He made an effort to lower his voice before saying more. "I've got people stationed out there to keep guard, and I've told them I'm going to pull the night shift. Can't be leaving the poor girl alone, plus it's a crime scene so we need to make sure it stays unsullied." Now it was his turn to pause for a moment. "I'd sure like your advice on this matter, Joe," he added cautiously. "Obviously we're going to identify the girl pretty quickly after we get her out of the ice, and I'm kind of expecting the phone to ring any second with a report about someone who's gone missing. I guess I just don't really know how to handle this. Sobolton's quite a safe little town, right?"

Joe opened his mouth to reply, before glancing at Pete; Pete, in turn, gave him a knowing smile before very conspicuously returning his attention to the glasses on the counter-top.

"You have to handle this situation with great care," Joe said after a few seconds, his voice becoming a little darker and more apprehensive. "Sobolton is my home, it always has been and it always will be. That doesn't mean I don't recognize little... pools of darkness that bubble up occasionally from beneath the surface. You have to kind of keep a lid on those pools, it's not hard but you definitely need to be aware of them and just... massage them away."

"What exactly are you talking about?" John asked.

"You'll pick it up in no time at all," Joe added, forcing a smile that was wholly unconvincing, even to himself. "You won't have any choice, not if you want to stick around. But let me give you one bit of advice that I didn't want to give you earlier, not when we were at the station and anyone might over hear." Even now he glanced around for a few seconds, as if he was worried that anyone other than Pete might be listening. "Don't ask why you see certain things," he continued finally, turning to John again. "Just massage them right away and then go on about your business."

"You're unnerving me a little here, Joe," John replied. "I think I have a right to know if there's something wrong or -"

"Let me stop you," Joe said, holding up one spindly finger. "You're already starting down the wrong path there, asking questions and wanting to dig at things. Never dig, John. Keep on the surface and you won't run into any trouble."

***

Stepping out of the bar, John stopped for a moment to look along the street. Somehow the snow was still falling, even though he'd assumed that by now the worst of the storm should have passed. Taking a moment to button the top of his jacket, John couldn't help but think back to everything he'd just heard in the bar from his predecessor.

"Don't ask why you see certain things," he heard Joe's voice repeating. "Just massage them right away and then go on about your business."

For a few seconds he wanted to turn around and go back into the bar, to make Joe admit that he was either pulling his leg or drunk. As far as John was concerned, no sane man could ever believe such nonsense, and he couldn't shake the feeling that some kind of joke was being played; after all, how could anyone swallow all that cryptic, foreboding nonsense that circled and circled without ever actually coming to a point? At the same time, John also knew that his best strategy would be to just stay on his own path and do things his own way; eventually the town would start to see that he was right.

"Do you know anything about wolves?" he'd asked Joe just before leaving the bar. "I hit something out there in the snow, on my way back into town. I think it might have been a wolf, although I'm not sure. Whatever it was, it took a chunk out of the bottom of my cruiser."

"There haven't been wolves around here for a long time," Joe had insisted. "It's possible one could have been passing through, but I'm pretty sure any packs were wiped out a long time ago."

"Lot of hunting and fishing goes on around these parts," the man behind the bar had added. "No wolf would last very long hanging around in the forest outside Sobolton."

The man and Joe had chuckled at that thought, but John wasn't chuckling now; he'd dropped his cruiser off at the station and asked Carolyn to get someone out to check the damn thing, but he felt that whatever he'd encountered out on the road couldn't have been a mere wolf; it had to have been something bigger and stronger, and more powerful, but also something that – at least from the collision, perhaps even from before – was seriously wounded. And while he didn't have much experience with wolves, John felt sure that a wounded specimen had to be bad news.

After all, wounded animals were always dangerous. His own son had proved that fact, long ago.

Turning and looking the other way, John saw the hills rising up high in the distance, towering above the horizon. Until that moment, he'd never truly appreciated the vastness and majesty of the natural world surrounding Sobolton, or the fact that the forest – snow-covered now and seemingly entirely inhospitable – was just as much a part of his jurisdiction as the town itself. He'd noticed that some people referred to Sobolton as a city, when it was nothing of the sort; now he sort of understood what they meant, because when the forest and the lake were included Sobolton certainly felt like a kind of metropolis. Staring at the distant trees, he tried to imagine the snowy land that lay out there, but he quickly reminded himself that there would be plenty of time to discover that world later. Besides, he'd moved all the way to Sobolton precisely because he wanted a break from the rest of the world; he was certainly getting that in spades.

"Sheriff," a woman said, nodding at him politely as she made her way past, dragging what appeared to be a home-made shopping basket. "Nice to meet you."

"Likewise, M'am," he replied, surprised by her friendliness.

"You're the new guy in town, are you?" a man said, walking past in the other direction but stopping to shake his hand. "Welcome to Sobolton. You're gonna really love it here."

"Thank you," John said, and now the man was already heading off, evidently busy with some task of another.

In that moment, John finally felt as if he was part of the town, as if he understood that he had a genuine role to fill. He'd understood that role already as an abstract concept, but now he felt as if he was slowly getting knitted into the fabric of the town. He could only hope that soon, when news broke of the little girl who'd been found in the ice, people would trust him to solve the case. And as he glanced around and saw various other people going about their business, popping in and out of stores on the town's main drag, he couldn't help but wonder whether at any moment one of them might suddenly let out a scream as they realized that they were missing a daughter or a sister or a niece.

Far away, the trees maintained their silent vigil over the town.

CHAPTER TEN

"DAMN IT!" LISA MUTTERED, reaching out to steady herself yet again against one of the trees. "When you get back down, Lisa Sondnes, you're signing up for the gym."

Taking a moment to regather her composure, she looked around. Aside from her own footprints, stretching back the way she'd just come, the space between the treetops looked entirely undisturbed. A thick blanket of snow had fallen, and more falling snow was creating a rustling sound as Lisa turned and looked the other way; in that moment, with the rifle still hanging over her shoulder, she felt as if she must be the first person who'd passed this way since the bad weather had begun. She was a fair way beyond the edge of the town now, and she was starting to realize the absurdity of trying to locate possibly a single wolf in such a vast terrain.

"You've never been much for the outdoors, have you?" she remembered her father having told her once, half in humor and half with a hint of disappointment. "Are you *sure* you want to follow in my footsteps and become a veterinarian?"

"I want to help animals," she'd told him defiantly.

"But how can you do that if you don't like their habitat?" he'd asked. "It's not just the animal itself you have to think of, Lisa. It's also the whole world around them, and the ties that bind them to the land. You won't just be dealing with cute little puppies and kittens. The life of a veterinarian is harsher than most people could ever possibly realize and I'm not sure you're up for it."

"Because I'm a girl?" she'd snapped back angrily.

Now, as those memories lingered in the back of her mind, she wished desperately that she'd been kinder to her father, that she'd listened to him more, that she hadn't reacted quite so vehemently against some of his advice. In the years since his death, she'd learned – and it pained her to admit this – that he'd been absolutely right about almost everything. He'd told her about all the challenges she was going to face, and while she'd dismissed the very idea of those challenges at the time, she'd found them all coming at her fast. The one area where her father had perhaps been wrong had been in her ability to face those challenges, since she'd clenched her fists and gritted her teeth and got on with the job. She wished now that she could see her father one last time and tell him that he'd been right about how hard the job would be, but a little off the mark when it came to her ability to cope.

"This is hopeless," she said now, looking around again. "There's no -"

Before she could finish, she spotted something dark near the base of one tree. She squinted to see better; she couldn't quite make the object out properly, but something lay half-buried in the snow. Figuring that she might as well take a look, she waded between the trees, huffing and puffing as her legs screamed with an aching pain. In truth, she almost turned back, but finally she reached the other tree and used her gloved hands to start pulling the twisted dark shape out from the pristine snow.

Sure enough, as she'd suspected, she found herself holding some frozen animal droppings.

As she examined the droppings, she realized that they certainly could have come from a wolf. The distinctive foul smell was absent, although that could easily have been because of the snow; the droppings were frozen solid, indicating that they'd been on the ground for a while now, and the canopy of leaves above had probably kept them from being entirely covered. Still, she figured that these particular droppings had to be no more than twenty-four hours old, otherwise there would have been no hope of them still being visible; they'd fallen partly under the cover of a jutting section of bark, which was the only reason she'd been able to find them at all.

Looking around, she once again saw the smooth layer of snow everywhere, but after a few seconds she realized that there might be some very shallow depressions in that snow, which *might* indicate animal prints that had since been almost but not entirely covered. Her mind was racing now, and she quickly took a small plastic bag from her pocket and slipped the droppings inside so that they could be analyzed later.

"You couldn't track a bull through a china shop," she remembered her father having told her once, in one of his worse moods when the pain had been particularly strong. "You haven't got the hunting gene."

She knew the droppings were most likely those of a dog, even if she wasn't sure why an ordinary dog would be out in the forest in such bad weather. Taking a moment to get her bearings, she realized that she was still on the lower slope of one of the hills, and that if she turned due south right now she'd end up at Drifter's Lake; she couldn't think of a single reason why any creature would go to the lake in such bad weather, so she turned and began to follow what she hoped was the path of whatever animal had passed the tree and left the droppings. As she waded through the snow, she reached up and touched the strap holding the rifle over her shoulder, just to be absolutely certain that she was still protected.

***

Around one hour later, having trekked much further than she'd originally expected, Lisa reached the crest of a shallow hill and stopped again to get her bearings. Having grown up in Sobolton, she had a pretty solid understanding of her location, and her only real concern was that she'd already traveled a little further from town – and from her car parked at the side of the road – then she'd intended.

Looking down, she saw some more shallow impressions in the snow. Something had *definitely* passed this way at some point fairly recently, although after a few more seconds she spotted a second and much more distinct set of prints crossing the path she'd been following, heading toward the north-west. These prints had clearly been left more recently; something had been walking on four legs through the snow within just a few hours, and as she glanced around again Lisa was suddenly struck by the realization that she was most certainly not alone. She instinctively reached up and touched the rifle's strap again, and she was tempted to hold the weapon in her hands for a little extra confidence although after a few more seconds she decided that might be an overreaction.

Reaching into her pocket, she felt around for a moment to check that she still had her cellphone and then she set off again, following the new set of tracks even as they arced up between the trees and deeper into the forest.

And then she froze, as she realized she could hear the sound of someone – or something – else moving through the snow. A fraction of a second later the other sound stopped as well, but she felt the hairs standing up on the back of her neck as she realized with absolute certainty that she wasn't alone.

Slowly, she took hold of the strap and moved the rifle off her shoulder, holding it so that she could be ready to fire. She looked back the way she'd just come, convinced that the sound had come from that direction, and somehow the silence she heard now only served to make her feel more unsettled. Looking around, she realized that she was in a relatively low position now, with snowbanks rising up on either side to provide perfect cover for any pursuer.

"You really shouldn't be in that position

right now," she heard her father's voice saying.

"Shut up," she whispered.

Turning to look all around, she waited for some tiny hint that might tell her which way to aim the rifle. A minute, perhaps a minute and a half, had passed since she'd heard any sound at all other than her own breath and the rustle of falling snow. Although the sound had been clear, she was already starting to wonder whether she might have been mistaken, and whether perhaps she was just letting herself become a little jumpy.

And then, slowly, she realized she could hear a growling sound.

She turned and aimed the rifle at the top of a nearby snowbank. The sound had already faded away, but Lisa's heart was racing now and she knew that the sound had been real. Trying not to panic, she took a step back in the snow, then another; she tried to take a third step, only for her right leg to catch on a buried root, sending her tumbling back. She tried to catch her balance, but instead she tumbled down the snow-covered hill before hitting one of the trees with her head. Knocked out instantly, she dropped the rifle; her finger caught on the trigger at the last second, firing a single shot helplessly into the snowy afternoon sky.

CHAPTER ELEVEN

HEARING A DISTANT BANG, John Tench turned and looked along the street. For a moment he worried that something might be wrong, but then he heard a second, slightly quieter bump and he saw that two men were trying to jump-start a sorry-looking old car in the nearby parking lot.

For a moment, this image of everyday Sobolton life captured his undivided attention. Here were two men struggling in the snow, trying to get the car running so that they could head off on whatever journey awaited; John watched as the men struggled and struggled, but he resisted the urge to go and help them. In that moment, still feeling like an observer of local life rather than an active participant, he merely wanted to see how the men would progress. A few seconds later the engine shuddered to life, and the men yelled at one another as they hurried to the doors and threw themselves into the vehicle.

The car bumped over the edge of the sidewalk and veered sharply to the right before sputtering away along the road and disappearing into the distance.

Looking at the door of the veterinarian's office, John saw a sign hanging on the inside of the glass declaring that the place was closed. He spotted a set of opening times listed on the wall nearby and realized that he was too late to see anyone, that the office had shut a couple of hours earlier. Sighing, he shoved his hands into his pockets and turned again, looking over at the nearby intersection and trying once again to get a feel for the character of this strange little town. So far, he'd come to the conclusion that Sobolton could be a quirky place, and he saw that as only a good thing.

Spotting a sign taped to a nearby post, he made his way over and saw a somewhat grainy photo of a swan, with some text underneath warning that the animal was a danger.

"I'm not sure swans are too violent," he muttered under his breath, shivering slightly as snow continued to fall all around. "Then again..."

Then again, what did he know?

"Sheriff?" a voice barked suddenly.

Turning, John saw an elderly woman

shuffling toward him along the sidewalk, seemingly unhindered by all the unswept snow. Something about her seemed unstoppable, as if – in that moment – no force in all the world could possibly have held her back.

"Are you the new one?" the woman continued angrily. "Are you the one who's replaced Joseph Hicks?"

"I am, M'am, yes," he replied. "Is there any -"

"Then perhaps you'll start taking things a little more seriously around here," she said interrupting him. "Now, I like Joe and I know he's a good man, but it's undeniable that he's been sleeping on the job for the last few years. I remember when he started, he seemed like just the guy we needed, but it turned out he didn't have a backbone. What are you going to do about that Stone man chopping down all those trees? He had no permit, he had no right to do it!"

"Well," John said cautiously, "I'd have to look into it and -"

"It's wrong," the woman continued, "that's what it is. Just because he's got money, he thinks he can do whatever he wants." Stepping past John, she tapped angrily at the sign on the post. "I don't care what he gets up to within the privacy of his own land, but he has no right to cause trouble for the rest of us. We're decent, law-abiding people and we have a right to be left alone! It's the arrogance that I don't like! The arrogance and the greed!"

She took a deep breath before letting out a heavy sigh.

"And the ignorance," she added. "I don't like the ignorance, either."

"Okay," John replied, still struggling to understand exactly what might be wrong, "I can tell that you're upset about something. If you'd like to make a report at the station, I'll be more than happy to look into it."

"My name is Susan Walpole," she said firmly, speaking as if she thought she was explaining things to a child, "and you'll find all my complaints have already been made. It's simply a matter of someone bothering to take them seriously." Reaching out, she jabbed him in the chest a little harder than he would have liked, although he had no intention of protesting. "I'm the last one, you know," she added. "Now that the rest of them are gone, I'll be having my say."

"I'm sure you will," John said as she turned and began to walk away. "Mrs. Walpole, I'd be happy to talk if you could spare some time!"

"It's not Mrs. Walpole!" she snapped back at him. "It's *Ms.* Walpole. Don't you know anything about this town? You need to brush up on things fast, boy! You won't last long otherwise!"

"I'm starting to see that," he murmured. "I

heard Sobolton could be a strange place, but this... this is something else." He glanced around, and after a moment he spotted a man wearing a cream overcoat and a gray hat staring up at the sky; following his gaze, John saw nothing of note, and he sighed as he realized that he probably shouldn't even ask. "This," he added under his breath, "is definitely something else."

***

"And you're saying it was a wolf?" Greg said as he rolled out from underneath the police cruiser, which had spent several hours now parked in the garage. "You're saying a wolf did this?"

"I said I *think* it was a wolf," John replied. "I've got to admit, though, that I don't have much experience when it comes to these things."

"I've never heard of a wolf that can rip open the bottom of a car," Greg countered. "I'm not saying it's impossible, but I'm also not saying I entirely believe it." He began to wipe his hands on a rag as he got to his feet. "Looks to me like the damn thing was almost torn open by some kind of can-opener. It's one movement, one big rip, rather than a series of impacts. Whatever did that was strong."

"I hit it," John explained. "I didn't mean to, obviously, but I'm certain I hit it with quite a bit of force. Then it just bolted out into the forest before I could even see it properly."

"Maybe it just woke up."

"I'm sorry."

"There's blood," Greg said, leading him around to the front of the cruiser and pointing at one side. "Not a lot, I get why you missed it, but there's some splatter there. But look at this." He crouched down and tapped the edge of one of the wheel arches. "Notice anything?"

"Some rust," John replied.

"Not rust," Greg continued. "I check every one of these vehicles myself, and I promise you that this cruiser was rust-free just last week. Besides, if you look closer, it's not rust at all. Instead, it's like some kind of acid, which I guess must have been mixed in with the blood or got sprayed at the same time or..." His voice trailed off for a moment. "Well, that's your job," he added. "Finding stuff out, I mean. My job's just to fix these vehicles whenever you guys bring 'em in all bent up. Call me crazy, but I'm getting the distinct impression that you're going to be keeping me very busy."

"What about the underside of the car?" John asked. "Is there any blood there?"

"Not a drop," Greg told him, getting to his feet again. "I really don't know what you hit, John, but my estimation is that it'd have to be bigger than any wolf. Couldn't have been a bear, could it?"

"I'm pretty sure I'd have known if it was a

bear. Do we have bears round these parts?"

"Not that I'm aware of."

"Good," John replied. "Let's rule bears out, at least for now."

"Great plan, but I'm at a loss to help you, because I've seen vehicles from actual traffic accidents that had less damage than this one. Whatever you hit was strong, really strong, and it hit back. It ripped open a hole under the cruiser like it was opening a can of sardines."

"And then it ran," John reminded him. "It didn't stick around for a fight."

"You should be glad. If it could do this to a cruiser, I hate to think what it could do to a human being. Can't patch them up the way you can patch up a vehicle." He wiped some more oil from his hands onto a rag. "It's gonna take me a few days to get this lady back into service, I've also got to fix some damage you caused with your little off-road excursion down to the lake." He stared at the car for a moment before turning to John. "Was that your first time driving in the snow?"

"I might have... struggled to adapt," John admitted.

"You could get one of the deputies to drive you around. Just until the weather clears."

"I'm a good driver!" John protested.

"Oh, of course you are," Greg replied, unable to stifle a smile as he looked at the cruiser again. "I mean, you've been on the job for about half a dozen hours, and so far you've only been involved in two accidents. That averages out to one every three hours or so, which... I suppose it could be worse."

"I'm a good driver," John said again. "I just had some bad luck, that's all."

"At least you bother," Greg replied, patting him on the shoulder before heading over to the desk in the corner, where he'd already set out the various items of paperwork. "Your predecessor had a much more relaxed approach to the job. He preferred to send his deputies out to see what was going on, and then they're report back to him, but I can already tell that you've got a more hands-on approach, which I happen to think should work out a lot better. You're not afraid to get your hands dirty, are you?"

"I don't see any other way of doing the job," John muttered as he checked his watch. "Speaking of which, I need to get some rest this evening before I head out to pull an all-nighter at Drifter's Lake."

"I heard a rumor that a girl's been found up there," Greg said, focusing on the paperwork for a moment before glancing at him. "A little girl, apparently. Is it true?"

"I don't want people talking just yet," John told him. "We're still trying to figure out who she is."

"Handle this one with care, Sheriff," Greg

added, with a hint of concern in his voice now. "People round these parts are used to the occasional pop of trouble, but a dead little girl... that's going to send them spinning. Looks like you've got yourself a real baptism of fire."

CHAPTER TWELVE

LETTING OUT A FAINT groan, Lisa opened her eyes and found herself crumpled at the foot of a snowy slope, leaning back against a tree. For a few seconds she wasn't quite sure how she'd ended up there, before suddenly everything came flooding back and she remembered hearing a snarling sound.

Filled with panic, she grabbed the rifle and stumbled to her feet. She was shivering in the cold now, but as she aimed the rifle up the slope she realized that at least she didn't seem to have been out for too long. She reached up and touched the back of her head, wincing as she felt a sore bump beneath her wet hair, and she took a cold deep breath as she told herself that she'd been completely vulnerable while she was unconscious. In that case, the fact that nothing had attacked her seemed like a good omen, although a moment later she looked down and saw more animal prints running in a line down the slope and straight up to where she was standing before extending back out across the snow.

Whatever was nearby, it had made its way over to her, perhaps even sniffing her before retreating again.

As her teeth began to chatter, Lisa kept the rifle raised as she looked around. All thoughts of inquisitiveness had left her mind now, and all she could think was that she wanted to abandon her plan and instead return to the car. She didn't even bother to dredge up any damning words from her father this time; she began to clamber back up the slope, aching all over but determined to get back to civilization and dry off. The new sheriff, she figured, could do all the actual hunting; she had the dropping in a bag and she supposed that once she proved they'd come from a wolf, she'd be able to get someone to take her concerns seriously.

And then, after a few more steps, she heard a whimpering sound coming from nearby.

Stopping, she looked around and saw nothing but more snow falling, before she realized that the whimper seemed to be coming from just beyond a rocky outcrop. Part of her really wasn't in the mood to investigate further, but after a couple of seconds she started wading over to the outcrop so that she could at least see what might be wrong. She had the rifle still raised, even though her hands were trembling, and finally she reached the edge of the outcrop and looked down to see an opening several feet below that had been partially covered by a wall of snow.

Inside that opening, something was moving in the darkness.

A moment later two little faces appeared, looking up at her, and Lisa was shocked to see a pair of wolf cubs. They were clearly young, just a few weeks old, and after a few seconds two more faces appeared.

"What the hell are you doing here?" Lisa muttered, looking around but seeing no sign of any parents. "This isn't the right time in the season."

Once she was sure there were no other wolves around, she began to climb down the side of the outcrop. She knew she was taking a risk, and that approaching the den could bring about a violent reaction from the pups' parents, but she couldn't help worrying that they'd been abandoned. She looked around again, just to be sure that she wasn't about to be ambushed, and then she headed over to the den's opening and dropped to her knees. Immediately, the four pups clambered out across the snow and made their way to her, seemingly pleased that they'd been found at last.

"Hey, little guys," she said, touching them with her gloved hands. "Looking a little thin there, aren't you? Are Mommy and Daddy not around to look after you?"

Sure enough, the pups appeared to be emaciated to the point almost of starvation. Knowing full well that wolves wouldn't usually give birth in the middle of winter, Lisa peered into the den and immediately saw a fifth pup, although this particular specimen was clearly already dead. She reached inside and pulled the tiny corpse out, holding it up, and she saw that it had died at least a week earlier.

"Poor guy," she murmured, as the four remaining pups scrambled desperately to climb up onto her lap. "One of you didn't make it," she pointed out, "but the rest of you... how long have you been left alone like this?"

She looked over her shoulder; something else was clearly in the forest and had left tracks in the snow, but she felt sure that the cubs' parents wouldn't have simply left them alone, which meant that something had gone terribly wrong. Besides, the tracks could easily be from some other predator, and as she looked at the pups again she realized that she couldn't possibly leave them in the den, where they'd surely freeze to death.

"I'm going to take you with me," she told them. "Don't worry, it might be a bit of a culture shock at first, but you won't make it out here by yourself, and I'm really not sure whether anyone's coming back for you. Either way, I can't take the risk."

Taking another plastic bag from her pocket, she winced as she slipped the dead cub inside. Once that was secure, she removed her jacket and used it to gather the four surviving cubs up, preparing them for the long trek back through the forest.

***

"Yeah, this is a car," she said a couple of hours later, as she leaned back out from the rear of the car and watched the cubs wriggling and squirming in her jacket inside the transportation crate. "You guys are clearly very young, so I'm guessing you don't have much experience with human things."

One of the cubs fell off the coat and hurried to the edge of the cage, trying to get through the bars.

"Not right now," Lisa told it. "You guys are thin and you're showing signs of malnutrition. If one of your parents is still around, they don't seem to be able to take good care of you, so I'm going to take you back to my office and help you get stronger. Then we'll see about finding a sanctuary or rescue center that might be able to take you until you get older. Does that sound like a fair deal?"

The cub at the edge of the cage pawed at the metal bar, while letting out another faint whimpering sound.

"I know it sucks right now," Lisa continued, "but this is the best thing to do in the long run. You guys..." She paused for a moment, watching as one of the cubs in her jacket struggled to even stand. "You won't make it in the wild," she added finally. "Trust me, you'll thank me for this eventually."

With that she slammed the trunk shut before making her way around to the front of the car and climbing into the driver's seat. Once she'd pulled the door shut, she sat for a moment looking out at the falling snow and wondering just what crazy situation could have left those wolf cubs in such dire straits; she was sure that at least one parent must be out in the forest, but her running theory was that for some reason this parent must have become incapable of looking after its children. Madness could do that, she reminded herself, and so could injury. She felt sorry for any wolf that returned to find its children missing from the den, but she reasoned that she had to do the right thing for the cubs.

Looking over her shoulder, she saw the crate shaking slightly and she heard the cubs crying out.

"I know it's scary," she told them, "but this is just how it has to be. Hold on tight and I'll get you to town in no time."

She put the key into the ignition and tried to start the car, only to find that the engine refused to turn over. She tried again, already feeling a slight sinking feeling in her heart, but all she heard from the front of the car was a persistent spluttering sound that seemed in no way promising. Muttering a few irritated thoughts under her breath, and wishing she'd remembered to get the car serviced on time before Christmas, she resorted to turning the key again and again, each time for a fraction of a second longer as she found herself wondering exactly what could be going wrong. Finally, just as she was seriously fearing the worst, the engine somehow capitulated and rumbled to life, leaving Lisa to lean back in her seat for a moment.

"Thank you," she whispered. "Thank you, God."

As she drove away, taking care to drive safely on the icy road, she was already trying to figure out what to do with the cubs when she got back to town and took them to the office. Lost in thought, she failed to notice the thin and bloodied wolf that was watching her car from the cover of the treeline.

AMY CROSS

CHAPTER THIRTEEN

A SMALL, WHITE TABLET lay waiting obediently in the palm of John's hand.

"You know this is all your fault, right?" he heard his son's voice hissing in the back of his mind. "If I'd had a better role model growing up, none of this would have happened."

Trying to clear that memory from his thoughts, John took a deep breath. He'd been hoping that the move to Sobolton might help him forget the past, and that strategy had seemed to work for all of about seventy-two hours. Now the thoughts were back, bringing his son's angry and mocking voice drifting back over the years.

"Mr. Perfect," his son's voice sneered. "Too busy being a cop to be a father. And now look at me, sitting in one of your cells. How does that make you feel, huh? Embarrassed? What do you think all the others are saying behind your back? Don't you reckon they think you're a bit of a failure?"

Slipping the pill into his mouth and following it with a glug of water, John told himself that he just needed to keep busy. He'd become something of a workaholic since all the trouble with his son, losing himself in his work as much as possible. The dreams were still a problem, of course, but that was why he really didn't mind taking a few tablets here and there to keep himself going; like a college kid pushing himself to stay up all-night so he could finish essays and prep for exams, John figured he just had to push and push and push, and that eventually everything would be alright.

He could feel the pill. Sometimes they went straight down, sometimes they took a while to move through the throat. This one was catching a little, so after a moment he downed the rest of the glass of water to help it on its way.

"Knock knock," a voice said, accompanied by an actual knock on the door.

John turned to see Joe Hicks watching him from the doorway, dressed much more casually than earlier with a white t-shirt cradling his belly and a Hawaiian shirt hanging open.

"Just thought I'd drop by and see how your day's going," Joe continued, stepping into the room.

"I tried to keep out of your way as much as possible, you don't want some ghost from the past hanging around. But I also thought I should be here in case..."

His voice trailed off for a moment as he looked at his old desk.

"Well, you know," he murmured, scratching the back of his head. "Truth is, I think it's gonna take me a little while to adjust to not being in charge around here. I'll get there, there's no doubt about that, but it's still... an odd feeling."

"Got a lot planned for your retirement?" John asked, glad of the distraction.

"Well, I -"

Before he could finish, Joe let out another muffled burp.

"Loretta's chili," he said with a sigh. "I oughta invite you over for dinner one evening, so you can find out for yourself what it's like. That woman damn near turns me into a walking bomb. I'd steer clear of it, but the damn stuff's just too good and I can't control myself. You come over and try it, and you'll see exactly what I mean."

"I'd like that," John replied, although he forgot to smile.

"So I hear there have been some complications with the girl out there in the ice," Joe continued, as if perhaps he was getting to the point of his visit. "Don't worry, I haven't been sticking my nose in or intruding, but some of the guys were talking earlier. She's still out there?"

"We're waiting for some specialist equipment that can't get here until tomorrow," John told him. "I've got guys sitting out there watching the site. I'm going to be taking the night-shift."

"I suppose that's all you can do," Joe replied. "Pulling an all-nighter at the end of your first day, though... That's got to be tough."

"I didn't come here for an easy life," John countered. "The world doesn't organize itself neatly into a nine to five pattern."

"That's true," Joe admitted, before letting out a heavy sigh. "I think you've got the right attitude, John. As far as I can see, you're gonna be just fine as the new sheriff of Sobolton."

***

"I give him six months," Joe muttered a short while later, sitting on his usual stool at the bar. "Twelve tops. The man's not from round here, he doesn't know our ways, he doesn't know how things work."

"Careful," Pete replied as he finished serving a guy over by the cash register, "if I didn't know better, I'd say you're sounding a little bitter and jealous."

"It's nothing like that," Joe said, clearly annoyed by the suggestion. "It's a simple statement of fact. I know I let things go a little while I was in the job, and I admitted that. I just think people overreacted, that's all. You show me a single sheriff in the entire country who does every little thing by the book, and I'll show you a sheriff who never gets anything done. The problem is, every so often people start to want to interfere, and then they don't show any goddamn sense."

Spotting some white flakes on the bar, he brushed them away.

"Still angry about being given the boot?" Wally Sourness asked from one of the other stools."

"I'm very much resigned to my retirement," Joe said firmly.

"So if something happened to this new guy," Wally continued, "and the town came crawling back to beg you to go back to work, you wouldn't do it?"

Joe opened his mouth to reply, before hesitating for a moment. He knew he should instantly dismiss the idea out of hand, yet he couldn't deny that some sense of longing was tugging at his heart. He was going to have to lie, he knew that for certain, but he was surprised by how hard the lie was going to be to drag out through his mouth.

"Absolutely not," he said finally, impressed by how convincing he sounded. "I'm done, Wally. I know when I'm not wanted, and I've got my pride."

"I heard there's been some business out at

Drifter's Lake," Carl Lobe said, having listened to the conversation so far from his usual spot in a nearby booth. "Anything serious?"

"Oh, you'll all find out soon enough," Joe muttered with a smirk, before holding up one hand in mock surrender. "It's not my place to say, and I certainly don't want to be accused of interfering in the new fella's business. When he wants to make the news public, he will, and nobody should be jumping in and doing that for him early. Lord knows, I want the man to have the best possible chance to hit the ground running. Never let it be said that I tried to sabotage anything." He looked down into his beer for a moment. "They found a girl out there, that's all. A dead girl. Little, apparently. A dead little girl."

"Who?" Carl asked, getting to his feet.

"Ain't for me to say," Joe replied.

"But do they know who she is?"

"I don't believe they do," Joe said, glancing around and seeing that he now had everyone's attention. He took a moment to appreciate the fact that he was important again. "Of course, John Tench being an outsider maybe would take a little longer to figure that out. He's not like one of us, we know the ins and outs of this town like we know the backs of our hands. There comes a point where a man gets a kind of sixth sense about to handle a difficult situation. Sure, sometimes the decisions are difficult, but you have to think about the bigger picture. I've always said, I'm willing to take some pain today if that means things are gonna be better tomorrow." He waved a hand in the air. "Or next year. A few years down the line. Whatever."

"He's got the deputies, though," Wally pointed out.

"If he uses them properly," Joe continued. "I'm not panning the guy, I'm not saying he's all bad. I'm just saying that he might not fit in here, and in six months or maximum a year he's going to figure that out for himself and head back south."

"If he lasts that long," Wally said darkly.

"Well, he's got to handle this little girl thing carefully, that's all I'm saying," Joe sighed. "A matter like this is gonna be highly delicate and would benefit from an experienced set of hands. Someone who knows how this town works. As it is, I can't shake the feeling that everything's going to get messy, especially when the girl's identity gets out. Now, I truly don't know who she is, but it's not my job to find out, is it? And somewhere in this town tonight, someone's gonna realize that their little girl's not come home. Or if not in this town, then close."

"Wouldn't they have noticed that already?" Herb Mitchener asked, leaning against the bar a little further along, having gravitated to join the guys from his seat in the corner. "What kind of parent wouldn't have noticed their kid's missing already?"

The others began to talk among themselves, while Joe simply sat and listened to them, smiling as he realized that he'd well and truly got the town talking. Sure, he might be the *former* sheriff of Sobolton now, but he could still stir things up and he certainly wasn't ready to fade away into irrelevance. As Pete wandered over and stopped on the other side of the bar, Joe looked up at him with an expression that seemed to be showing just a little sense of pride.

"I'm still important," he wanted to say, but he managed to stop himself just in time.

"Do you think this new fellow is gonna dig into old cases?" Pete asked cautiously, lowering his voice noticeably as the others continued with their chatter. "Do you think he's gonna look at stuff that happened in the past? Is he gonna want to dig up any old open cases?"

"I sure hope not," Joe replied, as a telltale flicker ran up one side of his face. "If he starts doing that, then we really *might* have a problem."

CHAPTER FOURTEEN

"THAT'S ENOUGH FOR NOW," Lisa said, moving the pipette away from the last wolf cub, smiling as the little creature tried to follow. "I know you're hungry, but I can't just let you take as much as you want. We have to have a little control about this -"

Before she could finish, the lights flickered. She looked up at the neon tube running across the ceiling, and then she turned to glance back across the room. Brian was still asleep in a cage at the far end, recuperating – hopefully – from his surgery earlier, but otherwise the office space was bare and empty. Lisa waited in case the lights might flicker again, and then she looked back at the four wolf cubs as she heard another faint whine coming from one of the poor little things.

"You're gonna be fine," she said yet again, as she carefully closed the gate on the front of their cage. For a moment she watched as they scrambled over one another, trying to find a way out. "I'm sorry your mom and pop weren't able to look after you. Obviously something went wrong out there, I don't know what but it must have been pretty bad for you to get into this state. The nurturing instinct would have been really strong for your parents, so for something like this to happen..."

She paused for a moment as she imagined a lone wolf returning to the den and finding the cubs missing. She knew the poor creature would panic, but she also figured that it had to be ill or crazy or both; looking at the window, she saw snow was still falling outside as the sun began to set, and she told herself that she'd done the right thing. She hated separating parents from their young, but at the end of the day she had a responsibility to protect the cubs.

"Can you make the difficult choices?" she heard her father asking, his tone indicating that he'd already answered that question to his satisfaction. "Can you do that, Lisa? If you really need to be tough, *can* you be tough? Can you be harsh?"

He'd certainly been able to make difficult decisions, and for a moment she remembered stepping out of his car one day and feeling a chill wind blowing against her face; she'd looked up to see a huge building towering over her, and she'd felt a knot of such terrible dread in the pit of her belly, and...

No.

Better not to think of that now. She caught herself glancing at a socket on the wall, but she immediately forced herself to look away.

One of the cubs let out a particularly sorry cry, and Lisa looked down to see that it was staring up at her with frantic, terrified eyes. More than anything, she wanted to lift it out of the cage and pet it for a while, but she knew that would be a mistake, that she'd only be forging a connection that would later have to be broken.

"I'm not taking the place of your mom, okay?" she said firmly, as the cub pawed at the bars in an attempt to break through and reach her. "I'm just your friendly neighborhood veterinarian, and my job is to get you well and find a recovery center or a sanctuary where you can grow up to become nice and big and strong. After that, other people will decide what to do with you."

Forcing herself to walk away, she headed to the door and flicked the light off, and then she looked back into the darkness. She could hear the cubs still scrabbling away inside the cage, and one of them was crying; she felt her heart starting to weaken, but somehow she managed to stay strong.

"You're not going to be here long," she

continued. "Two or three days at most, but don't worry. I'm going to find somewhere really good to send you."

***

"It's chaos here," Wade said, his voice sounding unusually clear over the tinny speaker on Lisa's desk. "I thought I'd be able to blow this place by now, but they need me. I'm not trying to big myself up as some kind of hero, but I'm by far the most qualified here and I can't just walk away. Not when I promised to do a job."

"I totally get it," Lisa said, clicking on the mouse as she brought up the website for another potential wolf sanctuary. "You've always been very conscientious."

"So it's gonna delay me by a few more days," he continued, sounding increasingly exhausted. "Babe, you know I want nothing more than to get back to Sobolton, right?"

"Yep," she murmured, opening another page and seeing some photos of one particular sanctuary.

"Babe?"

"What?"

"Are you listening to me?"

"Of course," she replied, "sorry, it's just that these wolf cubs are worrying me. I've got them on some proper nutrition now, but I really want to find them a good home."

"I guess we're both married to our jobs, huh?"

"They're so cute," she continued, "and despite their tough start in life, they're not really in any danger, not now that they've been rescued. They can grow up big and strong, and eventually they'll be released back into the wild. I'm just relieved that I was able to find them."

"So let me get this straight," he replied. "You went out alone into the forest, when you knew full well that there's probably a dangerous wolf out there. Is that the gist of it?"

"I had Dad's old rifle."

"Which you know how to shoot?"

"I know the basics!" she protested.

"It still seems reckless to me, Lisa," he continued. "So it wasn't about proving some point to the old man, was it?"

"This is part of my job," she said firmly, as she opened another page on the website. "It's not all... routine exams of cute little pet dogs and cats. Sometimes I have to get my hands dirty, just like Dad always reminded me." She clicked through to yet another page, before opening a contact box and trying to figure out how to phrase her message. "I was perfectly safe at all times."

"I believe you. Thousands wouldn't."

"It's getting late," she pointed out, glancing

at the window and seeing that the sun seemed to have set a little more just in the time she'd been speaking to Wade. "And cold. I want to finish up here and head home."

"Going anywhere first?"

"Like where?"

"I don't know, somewhere you could unwind a little." He paused. "I hate to think of you sitting home alone every night, with no-one to talk to."

"Well, if my boyfriend managed to get his butt home," she replied, as she started typing a message to the sanctuary, "then I wouldn't *be* alone, would I?"

"You know what I mean."

"I've never minded my own company," she said, focusing more on the message now than on the conversation with Wade. "Sure, I miss you, but I know you're coming back. And when you do, we'll make sure we get time to hang out. In a way, this is quite a healthy way of doing things."

She typed for a moment longer, trying to phrase things right, before realizing that Wade hadn't said anything in return.

"Are you still there?" she asked.

"I'm still here," he replied cautiously. "Just promise me you won't go marauding out into the wolf-infested wilderness again. Can you promise me that?"

"I promise nothing," she said with a faint

smile.

"I've got to go," he continued. "The guys are calling me, and I'll get ribbed to death if they think I've been on the phone to you for too long. Look after yourself, remember to take breaks from work, and above all make sure that you're in one piece when I finally make it back home. I really miss you, Lisa, and... there's something I want to talk to you about. Something I want to tell you. But I think it has to be face to face."

"Sounds ominous," she murmured.

"It's not, I promise," he replied. "It's something good. I think so, anyway. Damn, they're calling me again. I'll call tomorrow, hopefully then I'll have some more news on when I might be back. Kisses."

"Kisses," she said, although he'd already hung up and – in truth – she was far too focused on the message. She spent a few more minutes typing, then a minute or two to read through what she'd written and tidy it up, and then she pressed the button to send the message to the sanctuary.

Leaning back in her chair, she checked her watch and saw that the time was almost five in the evening. A kind of dark blue haze had fallen outside, although she could still see snow falling from the sky. For a few minutes she sat in silence in the office, wondering whether she should stop by the bar on her way home; Wade had been all in favor of that idea, but Wade didn't have a tendency to let one drink turn into ten, and she wanted to continue her recent trend of behaving well. She looked at her watch again, and in that moment she realized that a compromise might be possible.

After all, Milton's Diner would still be open, and technically that place was on the way home.

CHAPTER FIFTEEN

"COFFEE, PLEASE," JOHN SAID, sitting at a table in Milton's Diner. "And, uh... can you make it strong?"

"One strong coffee coming up," Wendy replied, turning to head back to the counter before stopping and looking at him again. "You're the new sheriff, aren't you?"

"At your disposal," he said, trying not to sound utterly exhausted.

"You know," she continued, "I think we're long due for a change around here. Joe Hicks was sheriff for a couple of decades and I'm not sure that's really good for anyone. I've worked her a long old time, and I see a lot from these windows. Even looking past all the rumors of corruption and stuff like that, a town like Sobolton needs a fresh perspective every so often, and I like the fact that you're from out of town. Where exactly did you live before you came here?"

"A little way outside New York City," he told her.

"Welcome to Sobolton," he replied, making her way to the counter. "One extra strong coffee coming up."

"Thank you," John murmured, looking at his hat resting on the table before turning to stare out the window. Snow was still falling, and he really didn't much like the idea of spending his night guarding the frozen girl trapped in the lake, but he knew that he had to lead by example.

A moment later, grabbing his phone, he tapped to bring up the office number and then he tapped again to call. He waited for someone to answer while watching snow falling outside.

"You're through to the sheriff's office," Carolyn said on the other end of the line, sounding a little bored. "This is Carolyn speaking. How may I help?"

"It's just me," John replied.

"And that is..."

"It's John," he said, surprised that she didn't recognize his voice yet. "John Tench. Your new boss?"

"Oh, right," she stammered, sounding a little panicked. "Sir, I'm sorry, I just don't have your voice quite burned into my mind yet. I'll remember in future, though."

"I'm heading out to Drifter's Lake in a few minutes," he told her, "and I know cellphone reception's a little patchy out there. So I just wanted to check one last time this evening whether there's been any kind of report of a girl who might have gone missing?"

"Nothing," she replied.

"What about across the state?"

"I took the liberty of checking already," she told him. "There's no-one missing. At least, not that's been reported, but... I don't see how that can be possible. You said she's only eight, nine or maybe ten years old, right?"

"Right," he said darkly.

"So someone *must* be missing her," she continued plaintively, with a hint of desperation in her voice now. "I don't know what's worse, Sir. On the one hand, is someone waiting for her to come home, convinced that she's just late? Or on the other hand, is there someone out there, some parent, who just doesn't care? Could she have gone missing, and no-one's bothering to look for her?"

"I honestly don't know," John said, nodding his thanks at Wendy as she set a coffee down in front of him. He watched for a moment as steam rose from the surface. "I've got to admit, I thought we'd have a lead by now, but hopefully we'll find something tomorrow when we get her up from the ice. This girl has to have a family somewhere, or at the very least someone has to be responsible for her well-being. I don't know exactly what's going on here, but I promise you, we're going to find them."

Spotting movement outside, he saw Joe Hicks walking along the road. Clearly a little worse for wear, Joe stopped and leaned against a post, as if he wasn't sure he could hold himself up properly, before continuing around the side of the diner.

"It's just not possible," John continued, "for this girl to have turned up out of nowhere. Someone has to be looking for her."

***

Around the corner, past the diner's main counter, Lisa sat looking at some print-outs she'd brought from the office. Although she'd sent a message to one wolf sanctuary, she figured there was no harm in checking out some more so that she knew they'd get the best possible care.

Glancing out the window, she saw a figure stumbling drunkenly around the corner. The figure stopped for a moment to steady himself against the back of a bench, and Lisa realized in that moment that this was the illustrious and supposedly respectable Joe Hicks. Having never really liked the man, she watched as he prepared himself for some fresh steps, and she realized that she'd been just as drunk – or worse – so many times in the past. In that moment, she felt a huge sense of relief at the fact that she'd managed to stay away from the bar that evening.

A few seconds later, hearing a faint buzzing sound, she turned and saw a power outlet on the wall nearby. She furrowed her brow slightly as the buzzing sound returned intermittently, and then slowly she leaned closer until her eyes was just a few inches from the socket. For a moment she felt as if she could sense the electricity behind the face of the socket, and she imagined the charge suddenly leaping out and attacking her face. A faint smile crossed her lips, and she couldn't help but think of so much immense power trapped behind those two vertical holes, waiting for the chance to reach out and grab someone by the brain and shake them and -

"Usual?"

Looking up, she saw that Wendy was making her way over. For a moment, startled by the interruption, she felt a little befuddled; she pulled away from the socket, sitting up properly and trying to act like a completely normal human being.

"Yeah, please," Lisa replied, somewhat startled by the promise of human interaction. "Definitely."

"You know," Wendy continued, "the day

you change your order and have anything other than that same coffee, is the day I think this whole town will fall apart. Your father was the same."

"He was?"

"Apparently all his life, he never ordered anything different in here. The first day I ever started here, one of the first things I was told was how Rod Sondnes liked his order."

"That sounds like Dad," she said with a faint smile.

"I miss that old fellow. He was a real gentleman."

"Yeah," Lisa said sadly. "He was."

"Except one time," Wendy added, "when we were out of so many things, and he had to have a black coffee, and I still remember the look of disgust on his face when he tried it. He damn near spat it out all across the table, and everyone else started laughing. He got kind of grumpy at first, but eventually he realized that he just had to go along with it. I always made sure to have enough of his favorite in stock after that, even though I'd only just met him, and he took me under his wing." She paused for a moment, as if lost in thought. "I'm sorry, you probably don't want to hear all this about him."

"No, it's fine," Lisa replied. "Honestly. I like the stories."

"Your dad was a big part of this town,"

Wendy continued, turning and heading back to the counter. "Let me just serve the other customer, and then I'll be right over with your usual."

"Thank you," Lisa said, slightly relieved to be left alone in silence.

For a moment she sat staring out the window once more; Joe Hicks was long gone, no doubt stumbling off into the night, and Lisa supposed that he'd get a dressing-down from his wife Loretta once he eventually found his way home. She'd always liked something about small-town life and had never entertained any thoughts of moving away permanently; she'd had to leave for a while so she could study, but she'd popped back at every available opportunity and eventually she'd taken over her father's surgery not long before he'd died. Now, sitting alone at the table, she pulled out her phone and considered calling Wade just so that she could chat to him, but deep down she knew she probably shouldn't disturb him. He'd be back soon enough, and she'd be glad to spend some time with him.

Hearing footsteps, she looked up just in time to see a figure leaving the diner. She'd barely even noticed that there were any other customers, but now she saw a tall man walking down the steps and heading away into the snowy night. For some reason that she couldn't quite figure out, she kept her gaze fixed on the man for a couple of minutes, until he vanished completely into the darkness. She hadn't recognized him, which was odd in a town like Sobolton where – as the only veterinarian, and as the daughter of a well-known resident – she'd come to know a lot of people.

But not all, she reminded herself. Sobolton wasn't *that* small.

Getting to her feet, and figuring that her coffee was going to still be a few minutes away, Lisa headed around the counter. There were no other customers now, and Wendy was busy wiping one of the tables.

"All these little flakes," Wendy muttered as Lisa made her way past. "I don't know what they are. Like snow, I guess."

"Huh," Lisa replied, stopping and looking at the far end of the table, then reaching over to pick up the hat. She glanced out the window, but the stranger was gone. "Looks like the last guy left his hat behind."

CHAPTER SIXTEEN

"OKAY, I'M HEADING OUT now," John said, as he started the cruiser's engine. "I shouldn't be too long."

"It's freezing," Tommy replied over the radio, and his teeth could be heard chattering. "I hope you bring some stuff you can use to keep warm, because it seems like we're in for another night of real bad weather."

"Yeah, I figured that," John muttered, steering the car around the side of the station and past the parked cruisers. "I'm still not leaving the site unguarded overnight. Have there been any developments this evening?"

"What kind of developments?"

"With the site," he said, slightly frustrated by the fact that he was having to remind his deputy.

"Has anything happened?"

"Just more snow," Tommy replied. "I've seen bad weather round here, but never quite like this. And never for this long. It's like this cold snap just moved in and refuses to let go."

"Yeah, well, I was warned the climate could get a little unpredictable up here," John murmured, glancing over his shoulder for a moment before turning to look again, "and -"

Before he could finish, the front right hand side of the vehicle bumped against the edge of the post marking the limit of the parking lot. Frustrated, John hit the brake pedal for a moment, before turning to see that Greg was smiling and waving from the large open doorway leading into the mechanic's garage.

"I'm not a bad driver!" John protested, even though he knew the other man couldn't hear him. "It's the ice!"

He watched as Greg headed back inside, out of sight; part of him wanted to go after the guy and press his point, but he let out a heavy sigh as he realized that there really wasn't any point.

"Yeah, ice is tricky," Tommy said over the radio, evidently having heard the whole thing. "You'll get used to driving on it, you just need to give yourself a little time. And you might not believe this right now, but in the summer the weather up here's gorgeous, it's almost like you're in a completely different place. Anyone can drive around on the roads round Sobolton in the summer."

"I'm not a bad driver!" John insisted, although he knew that there was no point letting his irritation show. "I'm on my way out there now, so just hold tight." He leaned out the window to make absolutely sure that this time he was clear of the post, and then he eased the cruiser out of the parking lot. "I don't know exactly how you guys used to do things round these parts, but now that I'm in charge we're going to do everything by the book. After all, a little discipline never hurt anyone."

Looking both ways along the road, he was briefly distracted by the lights of the diner in the distance. A woman was just in the process of opening the door and making her way out, heading down the steps at the front; for some reason the sight of this woman caught John's attention, and he watched her for a few extra seconds before realizing that he was wasting time. Changing gear, he drove the car out onto the street, only for the engine to immediately cut out.

"Are you kidding me?" he muttered, glancing in his mirror to check that Greg wasn't watching, while getting the engine running again. "If these cars were maintained properly, I might actually have a chance!"

***

A while later, with darkness having fallen, John climbed out of the cruiser, having managed this time to get it all the way down to the edge of the lake without any trouble. He was slightly proud of that fact and wanted to mention it to Tommy, just so that he could prove he was a good driver, although he supposed that making a fuss of this simple achievement would itself perhaps not look so great.

"Boss!" Tommy called out, waving at him from his position sheltering beneath the treeline. "Over here!"

"What are you doing standing out in the snow like that?" John shouted, wading over to him through the snow. "Why's your cruiser up by the side of the road?"

"Should it be somewhere else?"

"I thought you'd bring it down here so you could at least it in it," John said, struggling to make his way through the thigh-deep snow. "I didn't mean for you to sit out shivering all day."

"Oh," Tommy replied, "I... didn't think about that."

Once he'd reached his deputy, John turned and looked over at the icy lake. More snow had fallen, but he could just about make out the spot where the young girl lay trapped in ice; he felt a shiver pass through his bones as he thought of her corpse trapped down there, suspended in place, and he realized with a degree of frustration that the investigation really hadn't made any progress all day. Then again, there was a very good reason for that, and he felt confident that they'd hit the ground running once the body had been recovered.

"Did you speak to Doctor Law?" Tommy asked.

"Not yet," John muttered.

"He's the coroner round here," Tommy continued. "I'm not sure you're gonna like him."

"No?"

"He can be a little... abrupt."

"He's not the only one," John admitted.

"Well, you'll see tomorrow, I guess. So how's this gonna work, anyway? The guys show up tomorrow and cut her out of the ice, and then... do we thaw her out?"

"Thaw her out?"

John turned to him, but after a moment he realized that actually thawing her out was the next obvious step. In truth, he hadn't much considered the practicalities of the situation, at least not beyond the retrieval of the body, but he knew she couldn't be kept in the ice forever; there was blood frozen in swirls close to her, and he wanted to try to preserve that blood so that it could be tested, and he knew other clues might be trapped as well. Looking out across the lake again, he found himself wondering just how he was going to deal with the crime scene.

"I'll figure it out," he said finally. "I've got all night to come up with something."

"Are you really gonna stay awake until morning?" Tommy asked. "Aren't you tired?"

"I took a brief nap," John replied, "and I loaded myself up with coffee. If I do the same thing in the morning, I'll be fine. Besides, I'm used to not sleeping much."

"Is that because of your time in New York?"

"Something like that."

"I bet you were busy," Tommy continued. "I bet it was nothing like this."

"We didn't get too many frozen bodies," John acknowledged. "We got bad weather. We got snow. But, again, nothing quite like this." He paused for a moment. "You haven't spotted any sign of wolf activity, have you?"

"Wolf? Why would I?"

"I don't know," John sighed. "I hit something earlier, on my way back into town. I didn't really see it, but I'm coming round to the idea that it might have been a wolf. I should check with the local veterinarian to see if anything's been brought in. I can add that to my growing to-do list for tomorrow."

"I don't remember ever seeing a wolf in Sobolton," Tommy told him, shivering again. "This just doesn't really seem much like wolf territory."

"You never know when you might get a

stray or two," John replied. "I'm sure it's nothing, but I'd like to keep an eye on it, just in case."

"And did you make any progress identifying the girl?" Tommy asked. "I know we can't examine her yet, but have any missing girls been called in that match her description?"

"Nothing so far."

"Isn't that kind of odd?"

"It's more than odd," John told him. "I don't know, half of me's expecting to hear something overnight, and half of me thinks we should have received a notification already. I mean, who could be missing a child in this kind of weather and *not* report it? Sure, the parents could be incapacitated themselves, but then how did the girl end up here all alone? Something about this whole situation really doesn't add up."

"I'm sure you'll figure it out," Tommy replied. "If we're lucky, she'll have some kind of identifying mark on her body and then we'll be able to sort things out real quick. It's just the beginning part of the whole investigation that's getting all knotted up." He paused for a moment, looking out across the frozen lake as stars began to show themselves in the night sky. "The northern lights are really beautiful, aren't they?"

"The northern lights?" John replied, staring at the same sky. "I don't see them. I didn't think we'd be able to, not here."

"Oh, we can't," Tommy said, seemingly unperturbed by that fact. "I was just thinking, though. If we could see them right now, they'd be real pretty."

CHAPTER SEVENTEEN

"SO YOU'RE SURE YOU haven't seen those files?" Lisa muttered, with her phone tucked beneath her chin as she carefully moved another tottering pile of boxes from the shelves in her office. "I'm sure they were up here."

"Sorry," Rachel replied over the line. "I could come back in and help you search, if it's really that important right now?"

"No, it's fine," Lisa said, setting the boxes on her desk before taking the phone in her hand. She glanced at two electrical sockets on the wall before forcing herself to turn away. "I just feel like, now I know they're not here, I have to find them or it's gonna drive me nuts. You know what I'm like, I always have to have things in their right places."

"Okay," Rachel said, "but... I don't mean to

be funny, Lisa, but isn't the time like... almost eight o'clock?"

"So?"

"Do you have to still be at the office?"

"Don't give me a hard time," Lisa said firmly. "Would I be any better off, sitting at home alone? Would you prefer it if I was watching some lousy film?"

"No."

"Wade's out of town, and if I was home alone..."

Her voice trailed off; she didn't want to admit that she was scared of opening a bottle of wine by herself, although that was one of the reasons for her reluctance to head home. Another reason, however, was that she wanted to keep an eye on the wolf cubs for a few more hours, and she really didn't like the idea of leaving them all alone overnight. In fact, she was starting to wonder whether she should sleep in the office, just so that she could keep an eye on them. Sometimes she felt as if work was the only thing that kept her on the right track.

"Forget it," she continued. "I'm sorry I called so late. You can get back to whatever you were doing."

"Are you sure you don't want company?" Rachel asked. "I could be there in twenty minutes and -"

"Absolutely not," Lisa said firmly, before glancing at the open doorway as she heard a bumping sound coming from somewhere far off in the building. "Listen, I really should get going," she added. "Sorry again for calling, and I'll see you in the morning. If the files are still missing then, we can take a proper look."

Once the call was over, she headed out into the corridor and looked at the various closed doors. The bumping sound hadn't been particularly loud, yet she couldn't shake the feeling that it had come from somewhere inside; she walked over to the opposite door and pushed it open, and to her relief she saw that Brian was still resting while the wolf cubs were still trying to get out of their cage.

"Don't worry," she told them, "everything's in hand. I'm sure I'll hear back from the sanctuary in the morning. You guys are gonna be totally looked after."

She smiled, but a moment later she heard another sound, this time a kind of thud that seemed to be coming from the reception area. Closing the door, she made her way along the corridor and through to the small space behind the desk, but sure enough when she looked around she saw only a bunch of empty chairs. She flicked a switch on the wall, bringing the lights stuttering to life, but reception looked exactly as it should so late in the evening: there were no customers and no patients, and Rachel had done her usual exemplary job of tidying up before she'd left for the night. Still, Lisa looked around for a moment longer, just to be sure that nothing was wrong, until finally she turned the lights off and headed back to her office.

***

"Okay, so you totally *should* be right here," she muttered under her breath about one hour later, as she stood leafing through more paperwork on her desk, "but you're not, which means I've put you somewhere very clever."

Stopping, she looked at the various other piles she'd assembled.

"*So* clever," she added, "that I have no idea where they might be. Damn it, earlier Lisa, why couldn't you just used the standard way or organizing things that we've been so -"

Before she could finish talking to herself, she heard a distant knocking sound, as if someone was at the front door. She looked out into the corridor and froze, puzzled by the disturbance, although she supposed that someone might need some emergency help; usually there'd be a phone call first, but as she made her way around the desk she figured that something unusual might have come up. When she reached reception and switched the lights back on, sure enough she spotted the silhouette of a figure standing on the other side of the front door's frosted glass.

"Hello?" she called out, stepping over to the door and reached for the latch, before hesitating for a moment. "We're close right now. Can I help you?"

She waited, wanting to at least get some indication of the visitor's purpose before unlocking the door. After all, she had plenty of drugs locked away in various cabinets and she knew that sometimes people could get pretty desperate. She'd heard horror stories of robberies at other veterinary offices, and she had no intention of dropping her guard, especially since she was all alone late at night.

"Hello?" she said again. "This is the Sobolton Veterinary Practice. How can I help you?"

Again she waited.

Again, she heard only silence.

"If it's not an emergency," she continued, "you'll have to come back in the morning. We open at eight and one of us will be glad to assist you. Do you have an emergency right now?"

Still hearing nothing, she headed over to the desk. After glancing at the frosted window again, she tapped to wake the computer up, and then she double-clicked to open the camera feed. The computer was a little old and slow, and the system struggled to load the necessary program, but after almost a full minute she saw a grainy image on the screen showing a dark figure standing directly outside. Unable to make out any of the figure's features, she tried to zoom in a little, but this only caused the program to stutter and hang, threatening to crash. She waited, and then she waited some more, and now the image on the screen appeared to be frozen.

"Who are you and what do you want?" she murmured under her breath, waiting for the program to catch up to itself.

She looked over at the window again; from this distance, she couldn't quite tell whether the figure was still out there or not.

"Remind me to get a new computer," she sighed, returning her gaze to the screen. She clicked the left-button on the mouse several times, although she quickly realized that this was probably only making the problem worse. "Just as soon as I can find some money in the budget and -"

Before she could get another word out, the image caught up and the figure vanished in the blink of an eye. She looked over at the window again, and she felt a rush of relief as she realized that there was no longer anyone out there. Clicking on the program, she accessed several other cameras showing different angles of the building, and she saw that there seemed to be no-one in sight on any of the feeds. She had no idea who the person had been or what they'd wanted, or why they hadn't answered when she'd called out to them, but she knew from experience that people – even innocent, harmless people – could be extremely weird at times.

A moment later, hearing a whimpering sound, she put the computer back to sleep and made her way back through to the corridor. She walked calmly to the recovery room and opened the door, and to her surprise she saw that the four wolf cubs were frantically clawing at the cage, as if they were suddenly desperate to get free.

"Guys, that's not gonna do any good," she told them. "Are you even listening to me right now? Just simmer down and I'm sure I'll have news for you in the morning."

She waited, but they seemed particularly agitated, and after a few seconds she realized that they appeared to be trying to get over toward the window. Moonlight was shining through into the room between the heavy metal bars that covered the outside of the glass, and for a moment Lisa watched the window just to be sure that no-one was about to appear. The cubs were still whimpering, almost howling, yet the window itself remained completely bare and free of any spooky silhouettes.

"Okay, then," Lisa muttered as she swung the door shut. "If you guys want to tire yourselves out like this, it's fine by me. I'll see you in the morning."

CHAPTER EIGHTEEN

SIXTIES POP MUSIC BLARED intermittently over the radio, occasionally cutting out for a few seconds at a time, as John sat alone in his police cruiser and watched snow falling outside.

So far, in the couple of hours since Tommy's departure, John had spent his time sitting in the vehicle wearing a thick coat, trying to stay warm. Time seemed to be proceeding at a snail's pace, the seconds dragging past with a grinding lack of efficiency, leaving him playing a kind of game in which he looked away from the clock for a few minutes at a time and then tried to guess how many minutes would have passed; invariably he was always far too optimistic, but the game was almost keeping him occupied. He'd brought a couple of books along, titles that he'd been meaning to read for a while, but somehow he found that he really wasn't in the mood for reading. Instead, between rounds of the clock game he found himself staring out the window toward the far side of the lake.

A line of coniferous trees lined the opposite shore; at least, he thought they were coniferous, although now he wasn't so sure. He made a mental note to read up on the local area and to learn a little more about Sobolton's history.

Reaching into his pocket, he pulled out his phone. The time on the screen was the same as the time on the cruiser's dashboard, ruining his brief hope that perhaps there had been some mistake. He unlocked the phone and tried to bring up a website, only to find that the signal was far too poor. A moment later, as if to emphasize that point, the radio turned to a static wail that lasted for several seconds before the swirl allowed a hint of the song back through.

Spotting some items tucked into the phone's case, he pulled them out and found himself looking at a photo of his son and ex-wife. Their smiling faces beamed out at him from a sunny days many years earlier, reminding him of all the things that had happened since. His son, in particular, looked so happy and innocent as a young man, in complete contrast to the last time John had seen him face-to-face.

"Yeah," he muttered now, tucking the photo

away and slipping his phone back into his pocket. "That's just how it goes sometimes."

He glanced out at the lake again, and this time he couldn't shake the feeling that something was different. Snow was still falling, and the trees on the lake's far shore were still dark, but now John felt as if he was missing something important. He watched the scene for a few more seconds, convinced that he had to be wrong, and then he looked at the lake's closest shore.

And then, as falling snow partially obscured his view, he realized that he could see a figure standing on the ice, right next to the spot where the young girl's body lay frozen.

"What the -"

Opening the door, he scrambled out of the cruiser, instinctively checking for his gun. Leaving his hat on the seat, he slammed the door shut and waded through the snow. As he reached the edge of the lake, however, he saw that the figure on the ice had vanished in the blink of an eye.

He still raised his gun, however, while looking around for any sign of his visitor.

"Sobolton Sheriff's Department!" he shouted, his voice carrying further in the cold night air. "This is a crime scene! I need you to come out with your hands where I can see them!"

Turning, he aimed at the trees, although he knew no-one could have made it all the way over there, especially not in such heavy snow. After a moment he aimed at the lake again, but in his panic he was starting to think back to the sight of the figure; he hadn't seen its face, but her realized now that it had been fairly small, like a child, like...

Like the young girl in the ice.

Swallowing hard, he told himself to stay calm and to avoid overreacting. His heart was pounding and he certainly didn't believe that he'd imagined the figure, but at the same time he also knew full well that the human mind was capable of inventing things and embellishing details. A lack of decent sleep probably wasn't helping either, although he felt as if he was more than in control of his own thoughts. After keeping the gun aimed out across the ice for a moment longer, however, he began to lower his hands until finally he was simply standing alone on the snowy shore as snow fell all around.

"This is your last warning!" he called out, although he didn't really expect to hear an answer. "If there's anyone here, you need to show yourself immediately or..."

As his voice trailed off, he realized that most likely he was simply talking to himself. He waited for a few more seconds, just to be certain, and then he turned to make his way back over to the cruiser. After just a single laborious step through the snow, however, he stopped as he realized that he could hear a repeating sound coming from nearby, as if someone was tapping on glass. He turned slowly, looking out across the lake, and the sound persisted for a few more seconds before stopping abruptly.

"Now what?" he muttered under his breath. "I'm really not in the mood for games."

***

The little girl's body lay trapped in ice, exactly where it had been for many hours now, as John very carefully made his way out across the ice.

Almost slipping several times, John muttered a few curse words under his breath as he tried desperately to stay on his feet. He already regretted his decision to venture out onto the ice, but at the same time he knew that he had to make sure the crime scene remained uncontaminated. Already, he could think of half a dozen things he could and perhaps should have done differently, but after a few more steps he came to a halt as he saw the girl's body still encased in ice several feet below the spot where he was standing.

And, of course, she hadn't moved at all.

"Just checking on you," he explained, figuring that he should at least say something. "Hold on just a little while longer, young lady. We're gonna get you out in no time."

He waited, mainly as a mark of respect, although after a moment he looked around as he realized that something was a little strange. Snow was still falling from the sky, but none seemed to have really settled on the spot directly above the girl's body, as if for some reason this particular spot was determined to remain clear. Crouching down, he pressed a gloved hand gently against the ice and found that a very thin layer of water remained unfrozen across the surface; although he didn't have much experience with snow and frozen lakes in general, John felt sure that this was wrong.

Looking up, he watched for a moment as more snow fell from the dark sky above. Then, looking down, he saw that this snow seemed to melt away to nothing as soon as it landed on the ice directly above the girl's frozen corpse.

"Now what's that about, huh?" he muttered, before removing his glove and using one finger to tap against the ice.

He immediately realized that this sounded exactly like the tapping sound he'd heard earlier.

"A man could go crazy real easily in a place like this, huh?" he continued, staring down at the girl's frozen face. "Who are you, anyway? We're gonna find out, I can promise you that. You probably feel mighty alone and abandoned out here, but we're going to get to the bottom of this and we're going to find out who -"

Stopping suddenly, he realized that he could see a hint of red on one side of the girl's neck. Unsure as to whether that red smudge had been there before, he leaned closer to the ice; he peered at the mark, which seemed to be a cut of some sort, and as he squinted a little harder he realized that he could just about make out what appeared to be some strands of torn skin, as if part of her neck had been ripped open. Although he couldn't be sure, he was starting to think that once the girl was out of the ice, she'd turn out to have some kind of cut or wound around the back of her neck, and he couldn't help but wonder where else she might be injured.

"Was this an accident," he whispered as he pulled away from the glass for a moment, "or were you murdered?"

As the light cleared a little, he looked up at the sky just in time to see a hint of the moon emerging from behind the clouds. For a few seconds he felt as if the cold night air was making the moon shine extra bright, although he quickly reminded himself that he was far from an expert when it came to such things. What he knew about the natural world would just about fit on the back of a postage stamp, so as he got to his feet he figured that he really needed to avoid jumping to conclusion.

"I'll be just over there," he told the frozen girl, before turning and carefully making his way back across the ice, almost slipping with each and every step. "Not far. Don't worry, you're not alone out here."

CHAPTER NINETEEN

"SORRY," WENDY CALLED OUT, cleaning the filter on the coffee machine as she heard the diner's door swing open, ringing the bell, "we're closing!"

She reached into the machine and scrubbed for a moment longer, before hearing footsteps slowly making their way across the diner, heading toward the counter. Glancing at the clock on the wall, she saw that technically she still had a whole twenty minutes to go before she was allowed to lock the door, but she really didn't want to get into the mess of serving another customer. Besides, the coffee machine was all taken apart now and the last thing she needed was the hassle of another order.

Sighing, she wiped her hands on a towel before turning and heading around to the counter.

"Hey," she said, "we -"

Stopping suddenly, she was shocked to see a man standing on the counter's other side, staring at her with an unusually intense expression. Usually an extremely friendly person, Wendy found on this occasion that the man's face was somewhat unnerving; he was tall with straggly dark hair, and his eyes were noticeably bloodshot, while he was carrying himself with an unusual gait that left one of his shoulders a good couple of inches higher than the other. All things considered, the guy looked like he was extremely uncomfortable, to the extent that even his scruffy old clothes didn't quite seem to fit him properly.

"Hey," Wendy continued, forcing a smile as she tried to avoid caused offense, "I'm sorry, I've just turned the machines off to clean them so unless you're after something bottled..."

Her voice trailed off, and once again she felt extremely troubled by the man's gaze. After a few seconds, she realized that the hairs were standing up on the back of her neck.

"The bar down the road might still be open," she continued, making a point of looking over at the clock again even though she knew the time. "If you hurry, you should be able to get one drink before closing time."

She turned to him again.

"If you really hurry," she added cautiously.

"It's bright in here," the man replied.

"Huh?"

"It's bright," the man said again, before looking up at the electric light that hung down over the counter. Reaching up, he held the back of his hand close to the bulb. "But not very warm."

"Well, I turned the heating off too," she explained, still straining to sound relaxed. The last thing she wanted was to seem rude, even if this guy was giving her major heebie-jeebies. "I'm sorry, I have kind of a routine that I use when I'm closing up. I don't get paid extra to stay on after hours, you see, so I kind of have to get a lot of that stuff done before. It's not ideal, but I find it works for me and the boss doesn't really mind seeing as how we never get much in the way of customers this late. I'm not even sure why he stays open so long, except..."

As her voice trailed off again, she realized that she was starting to ramble.

"Are you... you're not from around here, are you?" she added.

"Not really," he told her. "I just sort of... popped down tonight for a visit."

"Funny time for a visit," she continued, forcing a smile. "I thought all the roads in and out of town were closed because of the storm."

"They might well be," he admitted, still keeping his eyes fixed on her.

Glancing around, Wendy was suddenly very much aware that she was all alone. She was determined to keep from panicking, to stay calm and composed, although she was also wondering whether anyone would hear her if she called out for help. She hadn't been working at the diner for *that* long, and Sobolton wasn't the kind of place that regularly drew visitors; she'd come to know most of the customers pretty well, and she'd certainly never had any trouble before. As she looked at the strange man again, her eyes were drawn to his hands and she saw that the knuckles of his right hand were smeared with some kind of reddish-brown substance, almost like...

"Oh," he said, evidently having noticed what she'd noticed, "I cut myself."

Holding his right hand up, he examined the smeared blood for a moment before rubbing it with a finger. Then, with no warning, he slowly began to lick the blood away.

"Right," Wendy said, still trying to make light of the matter. "So... like I told you a moment ago, I'm really just about to close up. But if you'd like something to take out with you, I'd be happy to see what I can find. Something nice and warm, maybe?"

***

His feet crunching in the snow, the man made his way from the front of the diner before stopping at the edge of the sidewalk and looking over at the dull lights lining either side of the road. In his right hand, he was holding a takeaway cup filled with the dregs of some instant coffee, but after a moment he reached over and tossed the cup – contents and all – into a trashcan.

A little way back, Wendy watched him for a moment from the door of the diner before double-checking that the door was now firmly locked.

Unaware that he was being watched, and clearly not caring, the man began to walk along the sidewalk. After a few steps he tilted his head to one side, stretching the damaged muscle running up from his shoulders. He winced a little, clearly in pain, but he kept walking as he passed various dark and shuttered storefronts. Already his eyes were fixed on one particular set of lights in the distance; past the sheriff's station and another row of stores, the low squat building housing the Sobolton Veterinary Practice was only partially lit this late at night, and the place looked empty and deserted. Stopping again, the man sniffed the air and waited for his senses to lock onto the distant site. Within a matter of seconds he'd picked up a mess of different scents, some familiar and some not.

A little way ahead, the door of McGinty's bar swung open and a very drunk man stumbled out. Having spent the entire evening drinking himself into a stupor, Wally Sourness was having to think very hard about how to stay upright, although after a moment he spotted the strange man still standing at the side of the road.

"Buddy!" Wally called out, waving at him. "Hey, you! Little late to be wandering around, isn't it?"

He waited for a reply, but the man ignored him, keeping his eyes fixed on the veterinarian's office in the distance.

"I don't know if you noticed," Wally continued, slurring his words as he made his way over, "but it's kinda cold tonight. There's this thing called a storm, and it's bringing this stuff called snow, and everyone's kinda shivering away."

He stopped and leaned on a post, watching the guy with a growing sense of amusement.

"You might wanna button up," Wally added. "You don't want to catch your death of cold, do you?"

He waited, but even in his drunken state he was starting to understand that something about this guy seemed a little different. A little off. A little... not Sobolton.

"I haven't seen you round here, have I?" he added, stepping a little closer. "You here on vacation? You sure picked a funny time for it. There's not much to do round these parts at the moment except... well, drinking's fun, I guess, but I've got bad news for you." He poked the man's shoulder with one outstretched finger. "McGinty's is closed for the night. Now, there's a store around the corner that's open all night, so I guess you could buy yourself a little something to take back to your hotel room. Where are you staying, anywhere? Sobolton's not really very touristy, so we're not exactly blessed with what you might call five star accommodation."

Again he waited, but after a few seconds he realized that this guy hadn't actually acknowledged him at all, that he hadn't glanced at him even once.

"I'm only trying to be friendly," he told the man, nudging his arm again. "There's no need to -"

Suddenly the man turned to him, and in that moment Wally instinctively took a step back. Something about the man's stare sent a shiver through his bones; he looked into the man's eyes for a moment and saw a faintly yellowish glow, and in that instant he was struck by a kind of primal understanding that he needed to get away. He mumbled something under his breath, some kind of apology, and then he turned and began to stumble along the sidewalk. With each step he felt his fear growing, until he passed McGinty's and stopped to look over his shoulder.

To his immense relief, he saw that the strange man had now disappeared. Figuring that he might just have had a lucky escape, Wally continued on his way, and he couldn't help but note that he now felt distinctly more sober.

CHAPTER TWENTY

"BUT IF YOU'RE LISTENING to this," the man on the radio said, his voice just about emerging from the undulating haze of storm-induced static, "then I guess you're a night owl just like I am. But don't worry, 'cause I've got the old hits to keep us both going all through the night."

Sitting in his cruiser, John stared out at the moonlit trees. He'd given up playing the clock game now and had simply accepted his fate; he was both tired and wired at the same time, struggling to stay awake but also alert to his surroundings. He glanced over at the lake again, still thinking back to the figure he'd briefly spotted, although he'd more or less accepted that this figure had been a figment of his imagination. While there didn't seem to be any particularly ominous shadows at the moment, he told himself that he was in a very unfamiliar environment and that it was natural for his mind to pick up on a few missed cues.

Hearing a beeping sound in his pocket, he pulled his phone out and saw a missed call. The signal out by Drifter's Lake was pretty poor, especially in such a terrible storm; he tapped to unlock the phone and saw an unfamiliar number that had tried twice to get through.

Staring at the number, he felt a flicker of dread. John Tench was not a man who answered call from unknown numbers, not these days, not on his personal device. He'd learned the hard way that certain people had a way of tracking down numbers even when they weren't supposed to; he'd changed his number three times so far in a matter of years, and he'd actually begun to hope that he'd done the job properly. Staring at this strange number now, he told himself that it was most likely some sales rep, or perhaps someone who'd dialed wrong.

Not *him*.

Setting the phone aside, he leaned back in his seat. The radio DJ had stopped jabbering, which John appreciated, and some old blues song had started intermittently playing over the speaker. Taking a deep breath, John briefly closed his eyes before reminding himself that he needed to stay completely alert; opening his eyes again, he stared out toward the trees and thought of the vast endless forest that seemed almost to encircle Sobolton completely, as if the natural world had never quite accepted that this town existed at all. Something he felt as if Sobolton was in danger of getting entirely cut off from the rest of the world, an idea that he had to admit contained some appeal. After all, he'd been trying to get away from everyone else for a long time now.

Everyone and their phone numbers.

Looking out toward the lake, he watched the spot where the girl lay frozen. Was she from Sobolton, or had she – like him – strayed into this strange little town? He couldn't help but feel a slight kinship with the girl; they'd both seemingly arrived at the same time, and they both apparently had no ties to anyone near or far. At least he understood why he'd ended up in such a state, and he supposed that it wasn't that unusual for a man of his age to make a break from everything that had come before. Something very different had clearly happened to the girl, however, and he kept coming back to the question of how nobody could be missing a child. Who were her parents? Why weren't they raising merry hell over her disappearance?

Sighing, he looked ahead, and then he froze as he saw the figure standing just a short way in front of the cruiser. He blinked, convinced that he had to be imagining things, but she was still there. Sitting up, he felt a chill run through his bones as he found himself staring at the very same young girl who he knew lay in the ice.

"What?" he whispered, as the girl stood in the snow and stared back at him. "How the..."

He hesitated for a moment longer, before opening the cruiser's door and stepping out. His feet crunched loudly and sank into the snow, and he felt the biting cold attacking his face as he stepped around the door and saw that the girl was still standing just ten or maybe fifteen feet away. Opening his mouth, he wanted to call out to her, but he wasn't quite sure what to say.

"You're dead," he whispered finally, glancing at the frozen lake for a moment before turning to her again. "You're dead," he said again, a little more loudly this time. "You're... you can't..."

His voice trailed off as he realized that her stare was intense, as if she was fixing him with some kind of very determined expression. Her skin was pale as ice but the area around her eyes was dark, almost black in places, and her irises seemed unnaturally light – as if the color had been frozen out of her. Now that she was free from the ice, John saw that the girl was wearing old and somewhat faded clothing, perhaps hand-me-downs, and that the sleeves appeared to be a little too long for her arms. As an icy wind briefly picked up and blew between the pair of them, John saw the girl's shoulder-length brown hair ruffling slightly, showing no sign that it was wet or frozen.

"Who are you?" he called out, still not understanding what he was seeing. "What do you want? Who... who are you? How are you here?"

He waited for an answer, but the girl showed no sign that she'd even heard him. Instead, after a moment, she turned slowly and pointed at the lake.

"I know," John continued, stepping toward her. "That's where you were. I mean... it's where you are. I mean..."

Again his voice faded to nothing. He wanted to believe that he was dreaming, that this couldn't really be happening, but he couldn't quite accept that any dream might ever be so clear and vivid. The girl was still pointing at the ice, at the exact spot where her body lay beneath the surface, and as he made his way over and stopped next to her John felt as if she was asking for his help.

He could also see that the ice remained undisturbed, that there was no way the girl – even if by some miracle she might be alive – could ever have broken free.

"Are you trying to tell me something?" he asked. "What is it?"

Looking down at her, he watched as she slowly turned and pointed in a different direction. Now her finger was aimed at the treeline on the lake's opposite shore, although when he looked in that direction John still couldn't see anything of note. Snow was falling, the lake remained frozen, and the entire scene seemed strangely calm and peaceful.

"I don't know what you mean," he continued, still watching for any hint of movement beyond the snowfall. "Is there something I'm supposed to be seeing?"

He waited, but after a moment he felt something icy touching his hand. He looked down just in time to see that the girl's other hand was touching him, and a shiver passed through his bones as her freezing fingers interlocked with his own; they were holding hands now, and although the girl was cold to the touch, John knew that he couldn't follow his instinct and pull away.

"What's that on your neck?" he asked, leaning back a little and seeing some kind of cut just below her hairline, with frozen blood all around the wound. "There's something on the back of your neck," he continued. "Did someone do that to you? Can you tell me who?"

As he looked down at the girl's face, he realized that she hadn't said a word yet, that she seemed to be almost lost in her own thoughts. She was still pointing at the distant trees, although after a moment she turned just a little more as if pointing to a different part of the forest.

"Yeah, that's not gonna help," John told her. "I'm sorry, but I need you to be a little more specific."

He looked down at the girl, just as she in turn looked up to meet his gaze; as she did so, her frozen neck cracked a little, and after a few seconds she raised her hand and pointed to the sky.

"Up there?" John asked, still struggling to understand exactly exactly what she meant. "The sky?"

The girl tilted her head slightly while still glaring at him.

"What's up there?" he continued, before looking up. "I don't see -"

Before he could finish, he realized that the sky had been replaced by what appeared to be a moonlit plate of glass. He blinked, but in that moment he realized that the 'glass' was in fact a perfect sheet of ice; when he opened his mouth to ask what was happening, he found that he could barely move at all, and he felt the sheer frozen temperature starting to bite at his face. Finally, realizing that he was somehow beneath the ice, frozen down there under the surface with the little girl, he forced his head to turn until he could see her again, and a fraction of a second later she opened her mouth and screamed.

CHAPTER TWENTY-ONE

SITTING ON THE FLOOR in her office, Lisa leaned back and let out a long, slow yawn. The yawn had been building for a while, and as she looked down at the various items of paperwork spread out all around her, Lisa began to realize that even by her own paltry standards this was a waste of time.

Glancing at the clock on the wall, she saw that midnight was going to roll around soon, and she could already feel the pull of her distant bed. Although part of her wanted to remain at work for a little while longer, deep down she knew that she had to go home to her empty apartment eventually, so she hauled herself up and headed over to the counter, where she stuck the kettle on to boil so that she could have one last cup of coffee before leaving. She waited for the kettle to boil, which seemed to take forever, and then she poured herself a cup of steaming hot instant coffee.

Heading to the little fridge, she took out a carton of milk and gave it a smell to make sure that it was still good. Then, making her way back over to the mug, she was about to add milk when she saw that there was no longer any steam rising from the surface. Confused, she set the carton down before leaning closer to the mug. Something seemed very wrong, and finally she carefully reached out with one finger and dabbed at the surface.

Cold.

Not just cold, but frozen.

She pushed a little harder, but somehow the coffee – which had been poured less than a minute earlier from a boiling kettle – was now a block of ice. She pushed again, just to be certain, but the frozen coffee in the mug remained completely solid. Unable to understand how that could have happened in the space of just a few seconds, she gave the mug a little shake before taking a step back.

"Huh," she muttered.

She paused, trying to come up with an explanation, but the entire situation still felt completely impossible.

"Huh," she said again, tilting her head slightly. "What the -"

Suddenly she heard the sound of glass

breaking somewhere down the corridor. She turned and looked through the open door, but already her heart was racing and she knew the sound could only mean one thing. She hurried to the doorway, and she listened for a moment as she tried to work out exactly *where* the window had broken.

Turning, she walked over to the desk and reached for her phone, before hearing the wolf cubs yapping excitedly. She froze for a moment, fully aware that the cubs were in a room without any medication, and slowly she looked over her head and watched the corridor again. She picked up her phone and walked back to the doorway, but now she could hear a voice speaking softly in one of the nearby rooms, as if somebody was talking to the cubs.

Swallowing hard, she stepped over to one of the closed doors and stopped to listen.

"It's okay," a man's voice was saying, "I found you. You didn't doubt that for a second, did you? I would never let anything happen to you."

Puzzled, Lisa listened for a moment longer before realizing that she needed to call the cops. Already wondering how the intruder had managed to bypass the security systems and the alarm, she turned and began to search on her phone for the number to the sheriff's station, telling herself that they'd be able to get along the road in a matter of minute before any -

Suddenly the door behind her shattered, sending her slamming into the opposite wall. The phone fell from her hand, clattering onto the floor; she reached down, before turning to see that a man was stepping toward her. Before she had a chance to reach the phone, the man grabbed her by the throat and pushed her back, lifting her up from the floor and pressing her so hard against the wall that she could barely breathe. She immediately struggled and tried to get free, but her feet were too high off the floor and when she reached up to grab the man's hand, she found that his grip on her throat was far too tight.

"What do you want?" she gasped, as the wolf cubs yapped and whimpered in the room behind the man. "All the medication is locked away and -"

"I don't want your drugs," he snarled. "Have you given anything to them already?"

"I don't know what you're talking about!"

"I know what your kind are like," he continued. "I remember how things used to be, and I'm sure they've only gotten a whole lot worse while I've been away. You shouldn't have gone interfering in my business. I had everything under control, I was dealing with her problems, I just needed a little more time. And then you had to come out there and poke your nose into everything!"

"I was only -"

Before she could get another word out, he threw her hard across the corridor, sending her crashing into the other wall. Letting out a pained cry, she fell down hard against the floor; she immediately tried to get to her feet, only to feet a sharp pain in her side. She spotted her phone nearby and reached for it, but the man quickly kicked it away, leaving to slide fast across the floor and hit one of the other doors. Lisa immediately began to crawl away, only for the man to kick her hard in the belly, winding her and knocking her down again.

"I'd forgotten how annoying this world could be," the man said, towering over her as she tried again and again to get back onto her feet. "I remember all the stupid games, but I'd truly forgotten the way that everyone just tries to get under everyone else's skin."

"I was just trying to help!" Lisa gasped, as she heard the cubs still crying in the next room. "I don't understand what you want, but I saved their lives! They were going to die and -"

"Enough!" the man roared, grabbing her throat again and smacking the back of her head against the wall, knocking her out cold this time and then letting her unconscious body slump down against the floor.

***

Opening her eyes, Lisa immediately flinched as she felt a heavy, dull ache in the back of her skull. She knew something was desperately wrong, but for a few seconds she couldn't work out what; finally, after blinking a couple of times, she realized that she was on the ground in the surgery's parking lot, resting in the snow.

"Come on!" an angry voice hissed nearby, accompanied by the sound of a car engine spluttering to life. Lisa immediately recognized that as her own vehicle. "Okay, that's better."

"What?" Lisa whispered, trying to get up but quickly finding that her body was too weak. She was freezing cold and starting to shiver, and after a moment she reached out toward the surgery's wide-open side door. "Help," she murmured, barely able to get any words out at all. "Somebody -"

"You're awake, huh?" the voice snarled, as footsteps crunched through the snow, approaching her fast. "That's a surprise, but I guess it can't be helped. You must be a little stronger than you look."

"Wait!" she gasped, trying to resist even as a hand grabbed the back of her collar and began to drag her across the ground. "Stop! Wait, somebody help me!"

She tried to grab something, anything, she could use to stop herself getting pulled toward the car. Although her vision was blurry, she could see a few lights in the distance and she told herself that someone had to be able to see what was happening; she tried to scream, but the pain on the back of her head was too strong and all she heard was a faint groaning sound emerging from her lips. A moment later she felt herself being hauled up off the ground, and before she could react she was turned around and shoved into the trunk of her own car. She tried to clamber out, but she was too weak to resist as the man pushed her firmly back down.

"Don't worry," he sneered as he held up her keys, which he'd evidently nabbed from the desk, "this probably won't be a long engagement for you. As soon as I'm sure I don't need you to keep the cubs alive, we'll be parting ways."

With that, he slammed the trunk shut. Lisa tried to cry out, but a moment later she felt the car starting to drive out of the parking lot, bumping over the snowy ground and then accelerating along the road.

CHAPTER TWENTY-TWO

"WAIT!"

Letting out a shocked gasp, John opened his eyes and leaned forward. Finding himself back behind the wheel of his stationary cruiser, he stared out at the snowy landscape for a few seconds before looking all around; the last thing he remembered was being under the ice with the dead girl, but now she was gone and he began to realize after a few more seconds that there was only one possible explanation. He'd been asleep.

"How was that one for you?" the DJ asked over the radio. "Okay, here's a little hit I like to call -"

Switching the radio off, John put his hands over his face for a moment as he tried to regather his composure. His encounter with the ghostly little girl had felt so utterly real that he still couldn't quite believe it hadn't happened; a moment later, feeling an intense cold sensation against one side of his face, he moved his hands away and looked at them properly. To his surprise, he realized that one hand – the same hand that had been held by the little girl in his supposed dream – felt positively icy.

He blew on his hands, and soon the proper temperature began to return.

"I'm losing my mind," he muttered under his breath, as he checked the clock and saw that the time was exactly midnight. "I've been on the job for less than twenty-four hours and I'm completely taking leave of my senses."

He sat completely still for a few more seconds, still feeling distinctly out of sorts, and then he looked out once more toward the frozen lake. Nothing looked wrong, the scene was exactly as it should be, yet he realized after a few seconds that he needed to check once again that the site was secure. Part of him wanted to remain in the comparative warmth of the cruiser, but after a moment he opened the door and began to climb out, while telling himself that he really needed to get his head straight again.

Suddenly he heard a snarling sound, and to his shock he saw a wolf standing barely ten feet away, baring its teeth at him.

"Okay," he stammered, instinctively holding

his hands up. "Let's be calm about this. I don't want to hurt you."

The wolf snarled again, while taking a solitary limping step forward. In that moment, John realized that the animal was injured, and that it seemed barely able to move one of its back legs at all. Thick blood was smeared across its matted fur, and more blood had dried and partially frozen around one side of its jaw.

"I think we've met before, haven't we?" John continued, as he began to very slowly reach for his gun. "Steady, let's not make any sudden movements. We met earlier today out on the road. At least, I'm pretty sure it was you. I didn't mean to hit you with my car, but -"

The wolf let out a louder, angrier growl, causing John to freeze with his hand just half an inch or so from his gun. He had no experience with wolves, so he really wasn't sure how quickly the animal could leap at him; sure, this particular specimen was injured, but that didn't mean it couldn't be deadly and he really didn't want to make the mistake of underestimating the natural world. He waited, trying to let the wolf calm down a little, before very slowly continuing to reach for his gun.

"You're a big guy," he added. "Or gal. Sorry, I'm not really sure. I'm certainly no expert."

Wrapping his fingers around the gun, he began to lift it up.

"This doesn't have to end badly," he told the wolf. "I don't want to hurt you. In fact, I'd very much like to help you. I believe there's a veterinary office just a little way from the station where I work, so if we can figure things out, I'd like to take you there and see about getting you patched up. Would you like that?"

He slipped a finger onto the trigger.

"Can we cooperate on that idea?" he asked, raising the gun until it was aimed directly at the wolf. "I really don't want to hurt you," he continued, suddenly worrying that by showing fear he might make an attack more likely. The animal was clearly injured, and possibly not right in the head. "I'm new here, as it happens. Not just to Sobolton, but to the whole small-town life. So if I come here and on my first day I end up killing a... a beautiful wild wolf, then that's gonna really set me off on the wrong foot."

He raised his other hand in what he hoped the wolf might interpret as a sign of peace.

"So let's deal with this in a pragmatic way, huh?" he added. "You back off a little, and I won't have to do the thing I'm really dreading."

Baring its teeth a little more and letting out a louder snarl, the wolf took another step toward him.

"I'm being serious!" he said firmly. "I *will* shoot you if I have to! I'm just begging you to please, please, for the love of -"

Suddenly the wolf lunged at him, opening its jaws wide and snarling. Startled, John instinctively took a step back and begun to turn away.

***

Snow continued to fall heavily, blanketing the forest as far as the eye could see.

A moment later a single gunshot rang out, echoing through the cold night air.

***

"Stop!" John shouted, slumping down against the side of his cruiser as he heard a loud, anguished whimpering sound. "Wait, hold on!"

Still somehow holding onto the gun, he watched as the injured wolf began to hurry away. Unable to run properly thanks to the fresh gunshot wound to one of its front legs, the animal slipped and stumbled in the snow, leaving thick patches of blood as it scrambled to clamber over one particularly high ridge on its way back toward the forest.

"You're hurt!" John yelled breathlessly as he got to his feet and brushed himself down. "Wait, you can't just run off like this! You need a vet!"

In a moment of panic, he'd missed his shot;

instead of hitting the wolf straight between the eyes, he'd hit the animal's upper front leg, blasting away a chunk of flesh and fur but leaving the wretched thing still able to run. He could hear a loud panting sound punctuated by whimpering cries of pain, and he realized that the wolf was liable to run off into the forest and die the slowest, most agonizing death. He checked his gun for a moment, and as he looked ahead and saw the wolf almost dragging itself between the trees he realized that he now had a duty to make its death as quick and pain-free as possible.

"Damn it," he muttered under his breath as he hurried after the animal, climbing over the bloodied ridge of snow and almost falling back down in the process. "Wait there! Wait!"

Once he was on the other side, he stopped for a moment to get his bearings and he realized that he'd lost sight of the wolf. He looked all around, seeing only the darkness of the forest, and he didn't much fancy getting lured into the wolf's terrain; at the same time, he could still hear occasional cries, and he hated the idea that the creature would struggle on in agony, bleeding to death slowly from the bullet-wound that even now had left it almost entirely crippled. Even in such a brief encounter, he'd seen that this wolf was a majestic animal, and he knew that it deserved a better death.

He also wanted to prove that he could do the right thing.

"Buddy, hey," he said, holding the gun up again as he advanced between two trees, ready for the wolf to jump out at him again. "I'm sorry, okay? I'm so sorry, that's not how that was supposed to happen. I let you down, and now..."

He stepped over a fallen log, still struggling in the snow.

"Now I just have to set things right," he continued, "even if that means... I get why you're scared, and I get why I'm not your favorite person right now. In fact, I get why you probably don't like people in general."

He made his way between several more trees, while looking around for any hint of the wolf. Although he hated the idea of putting the animal down, he knew that he had a duty. And then, as he looked around again, he realized he could hear a faint shuffling sound coming from somewhere nearby. Something was moving through the snow to his left, and he kept his gun raised as he slowly and carefully made his way closer. He told himself that he might only get one shot, that he really had to make sure this time that he ended the wolf's suffering. A moment later he saw the animal, limping round and round in a fairly tight circle around a patch of disturbed foliage that was just poking out above the snow.

"I'm sorry," John whispered, narrowing his eyes slightly as he aimed at the wolf's head. "This is for the -"

And then, before he had a chance to pull the trigger, he saw exactly what was resting in the foliage. His eyes opened wider again as he realized what the wolf had been protecting all along.

CHAPTER TWENTY-THREE

"GET OUT!"

A few seconds after the car had come to a halt, the trunk swung open. Before she had a chance to fight back, Lisa felt hands reaching down and grabbing her, hauling her out and throwing her down hard against the icy moonlit road. She let out a gasp of pain, and although she initially tried to sit up, she froze as soon as she saw a pair of legs stopping in front of her. Looking up, she saw the man staring straight down at her.

"What did you do to them?" he snarled.

"I don't know what -"

In that instant he kicked her hard in the jaw, sending her thudding back against the car.

"What did you do to them?" he asked again. "There's something wrong with them. They're acting... different, somehow."

"I took the cubs to my office," she replied, as she wiped blood from her broken lip, "and I fed them. I gave them a special mix of nutrition that's standard for this sort of situation."

"They're not acting like themselves."

"They're probably adjusting to being fed properly," she said, looking up at him again. "They're not used to it. It's not just a case of giving them the right food and liquids, then sitting back and waiting for them to get better. Their bodies need to deal with the change."

"You poisoned them."

"Of course I didn't poison them!" she hissed angrily. "Why would I do that?"

"You should have left them alone," he replied, turning and walking away for a moment before stopping and making his way back over to her. "They were fine, they just needed time. I had the situation under control."

"If you mean the den they were in," Lisa said, "then no, they weren't fine. They were freezing to death."

"You don't know what you're talking about."

"Actually, I do!" she said firmly, sitting up a little but not daring to make any sudden moves. "In case you didn't notice, I'm a veterinary surgeon and I happen to have a lot of experience when it comes to malnourished and orphaned animals! Those wolves had been left out there alone in the forest to die and -"

"Not true!" he shouted angrily.

"One of them was dead!" she replied. "The rest would have followed pretty soon after."

"They were being looked after," he insisted. "She just... their mother hasn't been well, that's all. She needs time to recover, but she's a good mother and she'll sort it out in the end. I've been watching over them and making sure they're okay, and I've been nudging her so she remembers how to look after the cubs." He hesitated, lost in thought. "You don't know much about them. Not really. How old do you think they are?"

"They're just cubs."

"Yeah, well cubs stay cubs for a little longer in my lineage," he murmured darkly. "There's not some arbitrary point at which they have to grow up. They stay cubs until they're *ready* to become adults, and that can take a while. Years. Decades, even."

"What are you, some kind of environmental activist?" she asked. "Don't you think you're being a little extreme here? What's so wrong with me trying to save those poor cubs?" She waited for an answer, and for a moment she began to think that maybe – just maybe – she was starting to get through to this crazed guy. At the same time, she was trying to remember whether she'd left her rifle in the back of the car. "We need to take them back down to my office," she continued, as she began to shiver slightly. "You obviously care about them, but I need you to understand that ultimately it seems like you and I want the same thing."

"She's had trouble before," he explained. "There have been other..."

His voice trailed off.

"If you're talking about this wolf's mother," Lisa said after a few seconds, "then I really don't know whether I can help her. There was an attack on a dog earlier today, the poor thing was pretty badly hurt and the owner thought the culprit might have been a wolf. If that's the mother of these -"

"She'd never do that!" he hissed, interrupting her.

"Pain can change an animal," Lisa continued. "So can fear. If she's no longer able to look after the cubs, then it's perfectly plausible for her to have become aggressive to other species. If she's suffering like that, the best thing we can do as humans is intervene and try to end her pain."

"Humans?" he spat. "Now you really *don't* know what you're talking about."

"We've got off on the wrong foot," she said, watching as he turned and looked over at the forest. She quickly glanced over her shoulder and spotted the butt of the rifle poking over the back seat, and in that moment she realized by some miracle that she had a chance. She turned to the man again and saw that he seemed not to have noticed the rifle at all. "How about we try to go for some kind of reset? Would you be open to that?"

"There's no reset possible here," he replied, before letting out a heavy sigh. "I have to find her, and I have to get the cubs back to her so she can see she's still a mother."

"The cubs are our priority right now," Lisa said, as she began to very slowly get to her feet. "Can we at least agree on that point?"

"They're not the first cubs," he murmured darkly, as a whimpering sound began to rise from the car's back seat. "I'm starting to think that I've made a mistake. If they're too weak to survive, then what's the point of going to all these lengths to keep them alive? You might have done me a favor by getting them away from their mother, at least now there's someone to blame. Meanwhile I can get her fit and healthy in time for the next litter, and then she can see..."

He paused, before looking up at the falling snow.

"I've tried to be a good father," he continued. "A good husband. I'm not claiming that I've ever been perfect. Far from it. But at least I've done my best, and I *know* that eventually we'll be a family again. Maybe that process won't be as a clean or as easy as I'd hoped, but..." He paused again, as if he was in some degree of discomfort.

"I'm sorry I dragged you out here tonight," he added. "I should have made things a whole lot cleaner. Those cubs perhaps aren't as strong as I'd hoped, but the next ones will be. Don't worry, though, I'll make this quick." He looked at her again. "You shouldn't be made to suffer, not now. I'm going to show you mercy."

"Let's take the cubs back to town," Lisa replied, stepping back around the car and looking at the back seat, where the cubs were wriggling and crying in a pile of jackets. "They can recover, you know. Sure, they were in a bad state before, but I've got absolutely no doubt that they can be nursed back to full health."

One of the cubs looked up at her with a mournful expression, as if begging her to help.

"I know what to do," she continued. "Give me two, maybe three days, and they'll be fighting fit. By then I should have heard back from the sanctuary and hopefully they can take them, and I'll drive them over." She watched the cubs for a moment longer, while trying to figure out exactly how to extract herself from the situation. The rifle was resting on the far side of the seat, unnoticed by the man, but she wasn't quite ready to lunge for it just yet. "You can come too, if you like," she added, hoping to get him on her side. "You can see where they're going to be raised, and you might even be able to arrange to visit them from time to time.

Would you like that?"

She turned and saw that he had his back to her now. Standing in the middle of the icy road, bathed in moonlight and with snow falling all around, he cut a strange and somewhat solitary figure.

"Well, you can think about it," she said as she began to reach into the car, hoping to get hold of the rifle. "There's plenty of time to -"

"Don't do that," he said suddenly.

She froze, with her hand just a few inches from the rifle as the cubs tried to jump up at her.

"Didn't you hear a word I told you?" the man continued, with his back still turned. "I promised to be merciful. To end your suffering. To put you out of your misery like the wretched animal that you are. If you look at it from that point of view, really you should be thanking me. So why don't you come over here and kneel down, and I promise that I'll make this so quick, you won't even know you're dying."

Slowly he turner to her, and to her horror she saw that his eyes were now thick and dark with swelling, oozing blood.

"The alternative," he snarled, as his normal teeth began to fold away, replaced by what appeared to be large, bloodied fangs, "is really not something you want to contemplate."

AMY CROSS

CHAPTER TWENTY-FOUR

"CUBS," JOHN MUTTERED, KEEPING his gun raised as he stepped closer to the spot on the ground, where the injured wolf was still walking round and round, circling what appeared to be some kind of open-air den in the snow. "But they're..."

Now that he could see the little nest-like structure better, he realized that it contained half a dozen young wolf cubs, all of which were clearly dead. They'd been partially covered by snow, but something – the mother, he assumed – had dug away much of that snow, leaving the little corpses uncovered and exposed to the elements. Bare and thin, and terribly emaciated, the dead cubs were curled up against one another as if they'd died trying to get a little warmth. They still had their fur, but they looked to be frozen solid so John really couldn't be sure how long ago they'd died, but the mother was clearly in distress.

"Your babies," he said, before letting out a heavy sigh. "Is that why you've been acting this way? You're trying to protect your babies, but... they've obviously been dead for a little while."

He looked at the wolf, and now she looked so much more pathetic; limping heavily, bleeding from the gunshot wound at the top of one leg and already injured from the collision from the cruiser earlier, she seemed to be entirely in a world of her own and John couldn't help but feel that her mind was shattered. In fact, he couldn't be sure what had come first; had the injuries left her unable to care for her offspring, leading to madness, or had the madness led to her failing the cubs, leaving them dead and thereby worsening her condition?

Taking another step forward, John saw that the frozen bodies were more rotten than he'd realized, and that they'd probably been dead for quite some time.

Suddenly the wolf turned and snarled at him again, baring its fangs as if it was about to attack. Raising his gun, aiming it straight at the wolf's head, John told himself that he had a duty to get the job done properly this time, and that for his own sake as well as the wolf's peace, he needed to shoot right.

"I'm sorry for what you've been through," he

said, "but -"

In that instant the wolf lunged at him, snarling and trying to bite his hand. He pulled the trigger, blasting the animal's face and sending it crashing back down against the ground. A brief, anguished yelp rang out, and John watched in horror as the wolf shuddered frantically against the snow. The animal seemed to be trying to get back up, even though most of its head had been blown away; after a few more seconds, however, this frantic struggle began to fade, and the wolf managed a few more desperate kicks and jerks before finally falling still.

Worried that in some way the creature might still be suffering, John stepped closer and stood over it, before leaning down and pressing the tip of the gun against its head. He pulled the trigger, blasting a bullet through the wolf's brain and making absolutely sure that its life was over.

"Rest in peace," he murmured, before stepping around the corpse and crouching down to get a better look at the cubs.

Using the gun's tip, he moved one of the frozen little corpses and saw that there were more bones beneath, as if the wolf had used this spot for more than one litter of cubs. He felt a rush of sadness running through his body as he realized that the creature had evidently been out of its mind, and he could only hope that – in its final moments – it had barely been aware of what was happening.

"Okay," he said, getting to his feet, "I think we're gonna have to find a place to -"

Before he could finish, he heard a rustling sound coming from somewhere nearby. He turned and looked deeper into the forest, worried that a second wolf might be about to appear; reasoning that the dead wolf probably had a partner, he raised his gun and aimed between the trees, fully prepared for another attack. He waited, and now the rustling sound had ended, but he couldn't shake a growing fear that perhaps somehow – from some direction – he was being watched.

"Anyone there?" he called out. "If there's anyone there, I need you to show yourself immediately, do you understand?"

Again he waited, but he was starting to think that the sound must have been caused by a gust of wind. He still looked around for a moment, just to be sure, and then he took another look at the dead wolf on the ground. Although he wasn't quite sure what he was supposed to do next, he knew full well that he couldn't simply leave her there to rot.

***

A few minutes later, struggling under the extra weight, John carried the dead wolf on his shoulders as he emerged from the forest. He had the dead cubs in his arms, too, and he was already thinking that he needed to show some mark of respect for the dead animals.

Stopping near the cruiser, he threw the wolf down onto the snow and then placed her cubs next to her, taking a moment to arrange them properly so that they were all together. Then he walked over to the rear of the cruiser and opened the trunk, and after rifling through the various items he took out the spare can of gasoline, giving it a quick shake to make sure that it was at least half full. Satisfied, he pulled out the emergency bag that was stowed in the back of every cruiser, and after rooting through the contents for a moment he found a set of firelighters.

"I can't bury you," he murmured, glancing over at the dead wolf and her cubs, "so I'm going to have to burn you instead."

Once he was back over by the wolf's body, he spent a couple of minutes dousing her and her cubs in gasoline. He glanced over at the lake a few times, just to make sure that everything was in order, and then he tossed the empty can aside and took out the firelighters. Staring down at the dead wolf, he found himself wondering exactly how she'd ended up in such a sorry state, and how she'd managed to let what appeared to be at least two litters of cubs freeze to death. He could only suppose that she'd been driven to madness, although after a moment he wondered whether the cubs' father might be around as well. Couldn't he have had some bearing on the outcome?

"This is 2024," he said with a sigh, as he took out one of the firelighters. "Apparently now we're all supposed to -"

Before he could finish, he heard the rustling sound again. He looked straight over at the forest, and this time he felt sure that something was out there, that something was watching him. He waited for any hint of movement, but the sound had already faded to nothing. The more he watched the forest, the more John began to think that no wolf would simply watch from afar, that any wolf – crazed or otherwise – would certainly have attacked by now. He still watched for a few more seconds, before opening the box of firelighters. As soon as he had a flame going, he dropped it onto the wolves and stepped back, watching as flames roared across the corpses of the mother and her children.

"Sorry I couldn't do more to help you," he said, although he was slightly glad to feel the heat from the roaring fire. "At least now you can... I don't know, you can rest in peace or something like that. I hope so, at least."

For the next few minutes he stood in respectful silence, feeling that at least *someone* should witness the funeral pyre. He could just about see the dark mass of the wolf in the heart of the flames, and he could hear the fire crackling and spitting as smoke rose up high into the snow-filled sky. Although he supposed that he should go back to the cruiser, John waited even as the flames began to die down, convinced that he had to do the right thing. He watched as the flames petered out, and now he could see the wolf's charred bones resting on the ground in a clearing created by a patch of melted snow. Feeling that he should try to say something to mark the occasion, he thought for a few seconds as he tried to find the right words, but deep down he understood that he'd already done his best.

Turning, he began to solemnly make his way back over to the cruiser.

CHAPTER TWENTY-FIVE

"WHAT ARE YOU... WHAT..."

Staring in horror, Lisa watched as the strange man took a step forward. Blood was leaking from his eyes now, and from his nose and mouth as well, and his gums seemed to be bulging strangely as the fangs protruded further past his lips. At the same time, he began to drop his left shoulder down, accompanied by a harsh cracking sound that seemed to be coming from somewhere deep within his body.

"You should have let me be merciful," he stammered, barely able to get any words out at all as his entire jawbone seemed to be on the verge of dislocating itself. "Instead you're... you're..."

Twisting his body around, he let out a gasp

of pain before lunging at the car, slamming against the trunk and stopping for a moment to steady himself in the snow. Startled, Lisa pulled back and clambered onto the back seat, and then she shut the door and took a moment to check that the car was locked. As the wolf cubs whimpered and cried next to her, she clambered between the front seats and grabbed the steering wheel, while looking around frantically in the desperate hope that the man might have left the keys somewhere.

Spotting the keys still resting in the ignition, she climbed into the driver's seat and reached for -

Suddenly something slammed hard into the rear of the car, lifting the back wheels briefly off the ground and sending the entire vehicle lurching forward by a few feet. As the back section slammed back down, Lisa was almost shaken out of her seat, and she heard a series of crunching sounds coming from somewhere near the front of the vehicle. She reached for the keys again, only for the car to shake even harder than before, shifting slightly sideways across the road as if hit by some immense force.

Looking over her shoulder, she saw the man stepping around to the other side of the trunk.

"What's doing that?" she gasped, before grabbing the keys and starting the engine, then reaching her foot down to the gas pedal.

In that moment, the car was hit by a third force, one that was stronger than the previous strikes combined. As the wheels began to spin, the rear of the vehicle rose up off the ground, and this time the entire car flipped over, crashing back down onto its side as the window next to Lisa shattered. Covered in broken glass, she let out an involuntary cry as she slumped down against what had been the roof of the car, and she heard the engine roaring briefly as the wheels spun hopelessly. A moment later the engine cut out, and Lisa turned to see that the man was now making his way around to the front of the vehicle.

The wolf cubs, having fallen from the back seat, were scrambling wildly in a mass of discarded coats.

"What are you doing?" Lisa shouted, watching as the man's feet moved to the front and stopped. "Stop! You're going to kill us all and -"

Before she could finish, the man stepped forward and kicked the windshield of the upturned vehicle, showering Lisa with more glass. She held her hands up to protect herself, but she was powerless to prevent several pieces cutting her hands and face. Screaming briefly, she saw a twisted hand reached through the broken windshield, but at the last second she manged to kick the hand away before throwing herself through into the back seat, almost landing directly on top of the panicking cubs.

Outside, the man shouted something that Lisa couldn't quite make out, as if his voice was struggling to break free from what remained of his jaw.

As the man walked around to the side of the car, Lisa leaned close to one of the broken windows and looked up. To her horror, she saw that the man's body was horribly twisted and contorted, to the extent that he'd even begun to rip holes in his clothes. A moment later he reached down and steadied himself against the road, and Lisa realized that his bones seemed to be trying to reorganize themselves, tearing through his flesh in places as the front of his face bulged out and huge fangs protruded from his mouth. His eyes were bloodied pockets now, leaking freely, and his skull seemed almost to be twisting around beneath the skin, becoming less and less human by the second and starting to resemble...

"A wolf?" Lisa whispered, barely able to believe what she was seeing. "Okay, this can't really be -"

Suddenly the man roared at her, cracking his jaw open to reveal huge fangs covered in glistening strands of saliva. The back of his throat was bloodied and swollen, and Lisa pulled back in the seat as one broken hand reached in and tried to grab her throat. As moonlight caught thousands of shards of broken glass, the hand grasped over and over again, each time falling just short of Lisa's face; each time the hand moved closer, however, she saw that patches of fur had begun to grow from both the wrists and the knuckles. A moment later the man's broken face – half human and half wolf – leaned down and peered into other car, screaming with a blood-curdling roar that almost burst Lisa's ear drums.

Bumping against the rifle, Lisa realized that this was her only hope. She pulled the rifle over her shoulder and fumbled to hold it properly. The car shuddered as the man slammed into her again, but as she turned to shoot she realized that she could barely see the man's legs properly now as he moved around the car. She could hear him growling and snarling, and she had to scramble back across the seat as she realized that he was about to attack from the other side. She raised the rifle and aimed, but at that moment the last remaining window shattered.

The man leaned down again, and Lisa saw in the moonlight that his body was horribly twisted, as if he was halfway through the process of changing from man to beast. In that moment, filled with a sense of panic, she could only adjust her grip on the rifle and then pull the trigger, blasting the man in the chest and sending him screaming and howling away from the car.

She pulled the trigger again, only to find that she was out of ammunition.

As a loud snarling and whimpering sound rang out, she searched through the upturned car, desperately trying to find any of the spare bullets she'd loaded earlier. The man slammed against the vehicle again, and a moment later the entire side door was ripped away and thrown toward the forest.

"Leave me alone!" Lisa shouted as she found a box of the silver-tipped bullets. She grabbed a handful and began to load the rifle, although a moment later she felt a hand grabbing her ankle.

Screaming, she threw her weight against one of the seats in a desperate attempt to keep from getting pulled all the way out of the car. At the same time, she swung the rifle around until it was pointing directly at the broken window, and in that moment she saw the tumultuous mass of churning meat and bone glaring in at her with pure hunger shining through its eyes as its jaws opened again to release a devastating howl.

Pulling the trigger, Lisa, shot the creature and sent it reeling back, and then she fired again before reloading the rifle. The monstrous beast returned for another try, but Lisa shot again and again, before reloading and firing twice more, each time bringing a cry of pure agony from the beast's chest. Although she could see *something* moving outside the overturned car, stumbling through the moonlight, Lisa had lost track of whether it was a man or a wolf or some awful combination of the two. She reloaded the rifle with her last two shots as the creature stumbled around the car, and then she shifted around so that she couldn't be attacked from behind.

The wolf cubs had scrambled into the front of the vehicle, constantly crying and warbling.

Raising the rifle, Lisa waited for the creature to attack, but in that instant she realized with a sense of dread that she'd lost track of it entirely. She could feel her own heart pounding in her chest, and she could hear her own labored breathing, but as she looked around she saw no sign of the man – or whatever he'd become now – in any direction. Figuring that she'd work out exactly what had happened later, she looked first one way and then the other, convinced that he was going to come at her again, yet somehow he seemed to have vanished into thin air. She knew she only had two of the silver-tipped bullets left, which meant that she couldn't afford to waste a single shot.

As she continued to wait, silence fell, save for her frantic breaths and the cries of the cubs nearby. Still looking around, she refused to believe that the ordeal was over, even as the silence seemed to settle and the sound of falling snow outside became a little louder. Lisa's grip on the rifle became a fraction weaker, and after a few more seconds she lowered the weapon a little.

Suddenly one of the front doors fell away, ripping from its hinges. Lisa screamed and turned, firing twice at the monstrous mass of flesh and bones that reached into the car; the figure pulled back and stumbled away, and in that moment Lisa realized that it had taken something. She clambered forward and watched as the figure disappeared into the forest, and then she looked into the front of the vehicle and saw that all the wolf cubs were now gone.

CHAPTER TWENTY-SIX

OPENING HIS EYES, JOHN realized that he'd been on the verge of nodding off. He'd been sitting in the cruiser for a while now, and the time was almost three in the morning. He blinked a couple of times, trying to keep himself a wake, and then he sat up properly.

"Damn it," he muttered, grabbing the flask from the foot-well of the passenger side and unscrewing the top.

His coffee was still warm, so he poured some out into the plastic cup and took a long swig. Sighing, he leaned back in his seat and waited for the caffeine to kick in; he still had three and a half hours at least until anyone else was going to show up, and then he had to somehow soldier on through the whole day. He was used to operating on a minimal amount of sleep, of course, and he knew he'd get the job done; at the same time, he was starting to wonder whether he might have slightly underestimated the demands of his new job. He'd never been sheriff before, and Sobolton seemed like the kind of place that liked to brood on a mystery or two.

Looking out at the lake, he began to question the -

Suddenly he heard something bumping against the back of the cruiser. He turned and looked, and then he checked the mirrors; he tried to tell himself that he'd imagined the sound, that his sleep-deprived mind was playing more tricks, but somehow deep down he knew for certain that someone or something had definitely hit the vehicle. He set the coffee cup down and opened the door, and then he climbed out into the snow and took a look around. There was no sign of anyone, and as he looked the other way he saw that the ashes of the burned wolf were still smoldering under endless snowfall.

"Hello?" he called out, but in return he heard only silence.

Sighing again, he climbed back into the car, determined to stay warm. He reached out to grab the handle, and he was about to pull the door shut when he suddenly spotted some patterns on the window's glass. Keeping the door open, he tilted his head, trying to read what seemed to be some kind of message, and finally he was just about able to make out two words.

"Help me," he whispered.

A shiver immediately ran through his bones. He knew that he'd have spotted that message earlier if it had been there. Climbing back out of the cruiser, he stepped around to the other side of the door and used one gloved finger to wipe the glass; sure enough, he found that the message had been written on the outside, although anyone standing in the snow would have had to have written it backwards so that it would be legible the right way from the driver's seat. He looked around again, wondering whether someone was playing a prank, and then he stared at the message again.

"Help me," he said out loud, wondering exactly when someone might have had a chance to write such a thing. "What in the -"

Before he could finish, he heard a sudden loud snorting sound. Turning, he looked all around, and the snorting sound seemed to be coming from every direction at once. He reached for his gun, convinced that another wolf must have showed up, but so far he couldn't set eyes on the damn thing. With the gun aimed and his heart racing, he began to make his way around the cruiser, convinced that at any moment a wolf was going to appear. He turned and looked toward the ice, and then he looked toward the forest, and after a moment he realized that someone was crouching in front of the makeshift funeral pyre.

"Hello?" he called out, puzzled as he lowered his gun and took a few steps forward. "Are you okay there?"

He squinted a little, trying to get a better view of the figure, but in truth he couldn't quite make him out properly; clearly this was a man, but his clothes were tattered and torn, and from behind the man's shape somehow seemed all wrong. John took a few more steps closer, and then he stopped as he realized that the snorting sound seemed to be coming from this strange visitor, accompanied by a scratching clicking sound every time the man moved his head. Sifting through the ashes and pieces of charred bone, the man seemed completely unaware that he had any company at all.

"Hello?" John said again, still holding the gun but not quite aiming it at the man's back. "My name's John Tench, I'm the new sheriff. Can I ask what you're doing out here in the middle of the night? Seems awful -"

Suddenly the man let out a louder snort, almost a kind of growl. He began to get to his feet, but John realized that he was struggling, as if he didn't quite have full control of his legs. At the same time, the man's left arm seemed to be hanging down very low, lower than John even thought should be possible, and he was starting to realize that this guy seemed to be not quite put together in the conventional way; sure enough, as the man began to slowly turn, John saw twisted muscles poking out from beneath the man's tattered clothing, and finally he saw a face that was neither man nor beast; two dark, bloodied eyes glared at him, set above a swollen mouth with large fangs jutting out at the edges.

"Did you," the man snarled finally, barely able to get any words out at all, "do this?"

"What happened to you?" John asked, taking a step forward before stopping himself. "Have you been in some sort of accident?"

"Did you," the man said again, fixing him with an increasingly angry glare, "do *this*?"

"My name is John Tench," he repeated, "and I'm -"

"She was sick," the man sneered, cutting him off, "that's all. She's been sick for a while now, but I've been looking after her. Every time someone from your world has tried to interfere, I've made them back off. *Every* time, I've managed to protect her."

"I'm not quite sure what you're talking about," John replied, resisting the urge to raise the gun but making sure that he was ready at a moment's notice. "Are you talking about the wolf?"

"She was a good mother!" the man hissed.

"The cubs... she did her best. I helped, they were strong and they were going to survive. This litter was going to be the one that survived. The others were too weak, or they were interfered with by people from your world, but this litter..."

His voice trailed off for a moment, and he seemed almost to be shaking with rage.

"Listen," John replied, "I think -"

"Why did you have to interfere?" the man screamed, taking several steps forward, even as John finally raised his gun and took aim. "Why do people like you always have to interfere? Why can't you leave us alone?"

"Let's take it easy," John said, keeping the gun up. "I need you to calm down and lower your voice, okay? Do you know anything about what's going on out here? Do you know anything about a little girl who -"

"We would have been fine long ago," the man snapped, "without your constant meddling." Tears were running down his face now. "I knew what to do, I would have brought her back, I would have driven the madness out of her. It wasn't here fault. It was never her fault. You're not from here, you're not from our world. You could never possibly understand."

"Why don't you try to explain?" John asked, still trying desperately to defuse the situation. "Why don't you start by telling me your name?"

"Why? So you can use it against me?"

"Friend, I just want to know your name," John said firmly. "Is that so bad? If we start with names, we can work our way out from there and come to an understanding." He looked the man up and down, unable to quite comprehend how someone with such obvious injuries could still be standing; he saw now glistening fresh blood, but he couldn't ignore the twisted muscles and – in some places – the broken bones jutting out from the man's body. "I think you need medical attention," he continued. "I can arrange that for you. I'll go to my vehicle and make a call, and then help will be on its way. Can we both agree that's probably the best thing to do right now?"

He waited, hoping that the man would accept his offer.

"And then," he added, wondering whether the guy might be on some kind of narcotic, "we can talk about everything else later. My priority is to get you to a hospital."

Again he waited, but the man was simply staring at him now. Although he felt far from certain that they were on the same page, John finally figured that he was going to have to make a move at some point.

"I'm just going to go to the vehicle," he said, before turning and stepping toward the cruiser. "That's all I'm doing. And then -"

"You killed her!" the man snarled. "I was going to save her, but you murdered her!"

"If you mean the wolf," John replied, turning to him again, "I only -"

Before he could finish, the man threw himself forward, slamming into John and pushing him hard against the cruiser's side. Although he tried to raise the gun and fire, John was powerless to resist as the man – showing terrifying strength – picked him up and threw him across the trunk, sending him crashing down into the snow.

CHAPTER TWENTY-SEVEN

LETTING OUT A SERIES of pained groans and gasps, Lisa began to crawl out through the broken window on one side of her car. She had to stop for a moment as her shirt caught on a shard of glass; the fabric tore slightly, and she took a few seconds to pull it free.

Crawling further, she stopped again as she felt glass cutting her thigh. Wincing, she turned and pulled back, and to her shock she saw that another shard had cut a hole in her pants; the sharp tip had broken through the material and had cut her leg, although when she examined the wound she found that the damage wasn't too deep. A few drops of blood fell onto her hand, but she quickly realized that she wasn't in danger of bleeding out.

Sitting on the icy road, surrounded by

broken glass as well as twisted metal fragments, she looked at her upturned vehicle and tried to make sense of everything that had happened. She still didn't understand what had happened to the strange man, who'd seemed to twist his convulsing body until it had barely seemed human at all. By the end he'd looked like some sort of monster, like an inhuman cross between a wolf and the dregs of a man. She knew that wasn't possible, that the moonlight and her mild head injury must have conspired to cause a hallucination, but she has no idea how the man had then managed to tip her car over onto its roof.

Touching the back of her head, she felt a sore spot, and when she checked her hand she saw fresh blood.

"Damn it," she muttered, starting to shiver again as snow fell all around, "when did -"

Suddenly hearing a growling sound, she turned and saw a wolf stepping out from the forest. She immediately pulled back and reached into the car, pulling her rifle out, although she knew she was out of shots. Leaning back against the side of the upturned car, she began to search in her pockets as the wolf slowly padded out onto the icy road and made its way closer.

"Hey," Lisa said, trying not to sound like she was panicking now, "do you mind staying back? I've just kind of... got out of something, and I'm not in a good state to be entering round two."

As she checked the rest of her pockets, hoping for a miracle, she couldn't help but be aware that this wolf was still very cautiously approaching.

"Hell," she muttered under her breath, once she was sure she had no more ammunition left, "this really isn't turning out to be my night, is it?"

She aimed the rifle, hoping against hope that somehow the mere sight of the weapon might be enough to deter the wolf. Keeping the barrel aimed at the creature as it continued to move closer, she realized that she could see what appeared to be dried blood around one side of the animal's jaw.

"Been in the wars, huh?" she continued, trying her utmost to sound calm and unafraid even though she wanted to scream. "You and me both."

The wolf began to make its way around her, treading through the glass while keeping its gaze very firmly fixed on Lisa's face.

"That's right," Lisa said, turning so that the gun was still aimed at the wolf's head. "There's really no need for us to get into an argument, is there? We're just two animals, really, out here on a remote road late at night when we should be tucked away somewhere safer." She swallowed hard. "A *lot* safer."

The wolf made its way past and approached the rear of the car, sniffing at one of the broken windows. Lisa flinched and began to pull away, although she was keen to avoid making any sudden movements. Every few seconds the wolf glanced at her, as if to check that she wasn't about to do anything, but its focus appeared to be primarily focused on the car's back seats. Leaning through the window, the wolf began to sniff a little more frantically and Lisa realized that it was searching for the missing wolf cubs.

"Are you after your babies?" she asked cautiously. "Were those cubs..."

She hesitated, trying to make sense of what was happening.

"I was trying to look after them," she continued, even though she knew there was no real point explaining herself. "This guy showed up... I don't know what his deal was, but he took the cubs and went off into the woods. I tried to stop him and to make him understand that I could look after them better, but..."

Her voice trailed off as the wolf turned to her and snarled. Realizing that the sound of her voice seemed to be driving this anger, Lisa swallowed hard and tried to come up with a better idea. She was still holding the rifle, and she couldn't help but wonder whether the wolf might have encountered hunters at some point, in which case it might well be wary of certain human weapons.

Slowly, the wolf leaned back into the car, pushing past the broken glass as if it was searching for the cubs.

Realizing that this might be her chance to get away, Lisa began to haul herself up. She was stiff and sore all over, but she seemed to have no broken bones so she began to limp around toward the front of the car. Her mind was racing as she tried to work out how best to deal with the wolf; part of her hoped that the animal would simply leave once it discovered that the cubs were gone, that it might head out into the forest and try to track the man down, but a moment later she saw that the wolf had already begun to climb out through one of the car's other broken windows.

"They're gone," she said out loud, before she could stop herself. "You have to believe me, I was doing everything in my power to look after them."

She began to back away as the wolf approached again, and now she saw that the animal's paws were cut and bloodied. Stepping on the broken glass, the wolf seemed not to care about pain or injury, and instead it sniffed the side of the car again as if it was still trying to work out where its cubs had gone.

"I don't know what else to tell you," Lisa continued. "I think -"

Suddenly the wolf lunged at her, slamming into her chest and knocking her down. Gripping the rifle with both hands, Lisa used it as a bar, pushing up to keep the wolf from her as it leaned closer; saliva dribbled from its open jaw as it placed its bloodied paws against her and held her down, and a low rumbling growl emerged from the back of its throat.

"Get off me!" Lisa hissed, pushing as hard as she could manage but finding herself unable to shift the animal at all. "I haven't done anything to you!"

The wolf leaned closer, snarling constantly now as more saliva dripped down and landed on Lisa's face. The harder she pushed back, the harder Lisa felt the creature pressing her down, and she was starting to panic as she realized that she had no way of wriggling free. She looked into the animals mouth and saw its bloodied teeth glistening, and she told herself that it had no reason to try to hurt her. And then, just as she was starting to brace herself for the animal to strike, she heard a distant howl ringing out through the snowy night air.

Immediately, the wolf turned and looked toward the forest. Its ears pricked up as the howl began to fade, but seconds later the sound returned with extra intensity, seeming to twist as it stretched on and on.

A moment later the wolf pulled back, stepping away from Lisa as if she was no longer of any interest. Relieved, Lisa pulled back against the side of the car, still clutching the unloaded rifle as she watched the wolf slowly making its way toward the middle of the road. The distant howl had faded away now, but the wolf was entirely focused on the darkness of the forest and a few seconds later the howl came back, louder than before. This time the wolf seemed even more interested, making its way forward and approaching the forest, then clambering up the slope and disappearing into the darkness.

Realizing that she might not get another chance, Lisa scrambled to her feet and took a couple of steps back. She looked all around, not quite believing that the wolf had simply left, but the distant howl returned a moment later as if some other wolf was calling out, beckoning its partner. Finally, filled with a sense of relief, Lisa turned and began to limp along the road. She knew that the journey back into town would take several hours, but she hoped that a passing car might offer a lift; even if nobody passed, she figured that she simply needed to walk as fast as possible and find her way back to civilization.

High above, a wolf's howl rang out once again beneath the glow of a full moon.

CHAPTER TWENTY-EIGHT

LETTING OUT A STARTLED cry, John slammed down against the ice with such force that he briefly feared the lake's surface might shatter. He felt a shock-wave rush through his body, but he quickly turned and looked back toward his cruiser, and he saw that the strange figure was already making its way over.

"Stay back!" John yelled, raising the gun that he'd somehow managed to hold onto when he was thrown away from the vehicle. "I won't warn you again! Stop right now with your hands in the air!"

He waited a fraction of a second, just to be sure that the creature wasn't going to listen, and then he pulled the trigger, blasting the creature in the chest.

To his horror, the creature briefly flinched but barely broke its stride, quickly stepping down onto the ice as it let out a loud, ear-splitting roar.

"Okay, that doesn't seem right," John muttered, stumbling to his feet and aiming again. "You're obviously a big guy, but everyone drops eventually. That's just a law of life."

He fired again, hitting the creature in the chest for a second time but still seemingly making no impact. Before he had a chance to take another shot, the creature rushed at him, swiping him off his feet and then lifting him up briefly before throwing him across the ice.

Landing even harder than before, John felt the gun slip from his hand and turned to see it slide away across the ice. He instinctively began to reach out, before feeling the ice shudder beneath his body as the creature made its way closer again.

Getting to his feet, John slipped several times as he tried to run, but a moment later he realized that he was close to the spot where the dead girl lay beneath the ice. He looked down and saw her dead face staring back up at him, and after a fraction of a second later the creature crashed against him from behind, letting out another roar as it sent him slithering and skittering across the ice.

Slumping down again, John realized that he was getting weaker and weaker. He turned to look over his shoulder, just as the creature swiped at him with one huge claw, cutting his arm and sending him crumpling back down onto the ice. Reaching over, he grabbed the top of his arm, but he could already feel that the jacket was torn and that blood was seeping through from the wound beneath. He flinched as he saw several drops of blood dripping onto the ice, and then – before he could react – the creature lashed out at him again.

This time the claws caught his chest, pushing him back and knocking him down onto his knees. He reached up and felt that the front of his coat had been ripped open; the claws had sliced into his chest, but once again the wound wasn't too deep. Trying to get up, he quickly dropped back down before slipping onto his side. Out of breath and losing blood rapidly, he felt for a moment that he might never get up again, and a few seconds later the creature grabbed him by the leg, lifting him up and then throwing him back down while roaring into the night sky.

As he landed, John realized what was happening. He was far from an outdoors kind of guy, but he'd seen enough nature shows to understand that sometimes predators toyed with their victims before finishing them off, and he had no doubt that the creature intended to finish him off. He tried again to stand, and again, but each time his body seemed unable to support him as he looked around and saw the gun several feet away on the ice. He knew his only hope was to get to that gun and find some way to drop the creature, but for a few crucial seconds he he felt as if he'd never be able to get to his feet again.

His flesh was weak, but beneath the flesh lay his bones, packed tight and so far unharmed. He tried one more time to stand, straining his muscles, before pausing for a moment; now his bones prepared to take the weight, tensing before slowly starting to work together, pushing and grinding and slowly starting to lift the drained muscles, forcing the body to stand even as John's brain feared that he might topple down again. Once he was on his feet, John's bones tensed again, holding him in place. Blood was still leaking from his flesh, soaking out under the surface of his clothes; the jacket was wrapped around him, and pinned to one section of the fabric there was a name badge identifying the human individual generally recognized by other people as Sheriff John Tench.

The creature lunched at him again, swiping its claws at his face, but at the very last second John ducked and threw himself to safety. Landing hard on the ice, he slipped and slithered several feet, passing the gun but reaching out and just about managing to grab it while he had the chance. Rolling onto his front, he let out a pained gasp as he held the gun out and looked up, and he saw the creature rushing at him again.

His first instinct was to fire at the chest again, but he'd done that twice with no great results so he hesitated for a fraction of a second. As the creature roared, bulging blood vessels seemed almost to be bursting from beneath its flesh, and John figured that these vessels might just be the weak spot he needed. He adjusted his grip on the gun, briefly changing his aim, and then he fired two shots, hitting the side of the creature's neck both times and obliterating the flesh.

Immediately, the creature dropped down onto all fours. Blood was gushing from the wound in its neck; letting out a pained cry, the creature reached up with one half-human hand and tried to stem the flow, but already more and more blood was splattering down onto the ice. And as John stared, trying to work out where to aim next, he realized that this blood was doing more than just covering the surface of the frozen lake; somehow the blood was fizzing and sizzling, burning through the ice and causing cracks to start snaking out beneath the creature's stumbling, writhing body. As more blood spilled out, the fizzing continued, seemingly melting the ice even as the creature tried again and again and again to get back on its feet.

Getting to his feet, John almost slipped several times but finally he managed to stay upright, while keeping the gun very much aimed at the flailing creature.

Letting out another cry, this one tinged with fear and pain, the creature tried yet again to stand. This time part of the ice beneath its body cracked open, dropping its back legs into the cold water beneath the surface. The creature was clearly panicking now, desperately trying to drag itself back out onto the collapsing ice. John's first thought was that he should find some way to help, but a moment later he realized that the ice beneath his own body was starting to weaken, and he had no choice but to pull a little further back.

Howling as it began to slip deeper into the water, the creature reached out and dug its claws deep into the ice. For a moment this seemed to be working, but soon its claws began to slip free and the ice disintegrated, and the creature's entire body fell deeper into the lake until only its head and one arm were visible. The howling sound became more feverish, stuttering as if the creature was shivering to death, and gradually its attempts to pull free became less and less frantic. Finally the claws dug into the ice one final time, before slipping almost immediately as the creature's great hulking body tipped down beneath the surface, vanishing into the depths and leaving only a handful of bubbles on the surface. Soon these bubble burst, and now all that remained was a gaping hole in the ice.

Still bleeding from several wounds, John stared at the hole for a few seconds before getting up and turning to start limping back to the shore. He saw that the dead girl was still trapped in the ice, and he kept walking until finally he reached the shore and managed – almost on all fours – to scramble to the cruiser. Pulling the door open, he threw himself inside and lay on the front seats for a moment, before grabbing the radio and holding down the button on the side.

"Sheriff, what's up?" the night shift operator asked. "I was just about to give you a call to check up on things. How are you doing out there? Got anything much to report?"

AMY CROSS

CHAPTER TWENTY-NINE

STANDING IN THE CORRIDOR, Lisa stared down at all the broken glass that lay on the floor. She'd already checked the rest of the surgery and nothing was missing, although curiously the cameras had all managed to fail shortly before her abduction, meaning that she was short on actual evidence.

Limping through into the back room, she made her way over to Brian and saw that he was starting to slowly wake up. She saw his tired, still slightly drugged eyes staring at her, and she reached out and gently stroked his side, while taking care to avoid disturbing any of his stitches.

"Hey there," she said slightly weakly, still feeling as if she might faint at any moment. "Welcome back to the land of the living."

Placing the back of her hand against his nose, she felt a faint impression of moisture.

"You're doing better than I dared hope," she continued. "You're not out of the woods yet, and I'm going to have to keep you in for observation for a while, but hopefully within a day or two you'll be ready to go home." She stroked him for a moment longer, before hearing the telltale sound of keys unlocking the front door, which could only mean one thing. "I'll be back soon," she told the sleepy animal. "You've been really lucky, Brian. I hope you know that."

Making her way out into the corridor, she headed to reception and arrived just in time to see Rachel standing at the counter, looking around at the mess.

"Long night," Lisa told her.

"What happened?" Rachel asked, clearly shocked. "Was there a break-in? Wait, you look awful, did you get attacked?"

"A werewolf showed up and stole the wolf cubs, and he kidnapped me and wrecked my car before I managed to fight back by shooting him with..." She paused as she thought back to the events of the previous night. "Silver bullets, as it happens. Huh. I wonder why Dad had those."

"A what did what do you?" Rachel stammered.

"Nothing," Lisa replied, shaking her head.

"Sorry, I still need to get my head straight. Can you reschedule all my appointments for the next couple of hours? I don't think there's anything urgent in the book, and I kind of need a little time to figure all of this out." She made her way toward the front door. "First things first, I have to get someone to go and haul my car back to town. Then I need to go to the sheriff's office and file a report, and make sure the new guy has read everything I left on his desk." Stopping at the open door, she turned to Rachel again. "I haven't met the new guy yet. I hope he's... open-minded about these things."

"You haven't been drinking, have you?" Rachel replied cautiously. "It's okay if you have, I won't judge you, it's just... I remember what it was like working here when your father..."

"No, I haven't been drinking," Lisa told her, and she actually managed a very faint smile. "Don't worry, I'm not going to turn into him."

With that she headed outside, still limping slightly but otherwise mostly unharmed from her adventures during the night. Stopping at the edge of the parking lot, she looked across the street and saw that McGinty's was already opening up, ready for the early trade. For a few seconds she wondered whether a beer might make her feel better, but deep down she knew that would be a mistake. She'd never been a heavy drinker, she'd never even been drunk, but she knew the alcoholic genes ran deep in her family and she was too scared to risk giving them a poke. The last thing she wanted was to become some kind of cliched, stereotypical heavy drinker.

Besides, she had work to do.

***

"Lift!" a voice called out over the sound of grinding heavy machinery, and the ice creaked and groaned as the crane began to pull back. "Keep going! Don't stop now!"

Leaning against the hood of his cruiser, with morning light almost blinding him as it stretched across the lake, John Tench watched a chunk of ice slowly rising from the frozen water. He could see a dark smudge in the ice, and he knew that finally he might soon start to get a few answers about the girl who'd been found trapped; he still wasn't entirely sure that this was the best approach, and he worried about contaminating the crime scene, but he also knew that the girl couldn't just be left down there in the ice until spring. All things considered, then, this felt like the best approach to take in the circumstances.

"Gonna take a while to thaw her out," a voice said, and John turned to see an elderly man making his way over. "I might not be able to start the autopsy for another few hours."

The man paused for a moment, leaning heavily on a cane, before holding out a hand.

"Doctor Robert Law," he continued, as John shook his outstretched hand. "One of the many hats I wear around this town is that of the local coroner. Do you trust me to carry out the autopsy, or are you going to insist on bringing in someone from outside the town?"

"I look forward to reading your report," John replied.

"It's a hell of a case," Law muttered, turning to watch as the block of ice containing the girl was swung toward the shoreline. "I've carried out a fair few autopsies over the years, but I'm not sure I've ever had to defrost anyone first. I'm not even sure of the protocol involved, although I suppose I should save the water once it's melted."

"That might be a good idea," John told him.

"I spoke to Tommy," Law added. "He says you still don't know who this girl is. Apparently there have been no reports of anyone missing." He looked John up and down for a moment. "Well, you'll have to forgive my manners," he added, "but I only just noticed. Man, you look absolutely terrible, like you've been through the wringer and then some. Are you sure you shouldn't get yourself checked out at the hospital?"

"I'll go when I get a chance," John murmured, as he continued to watch the block containing the dead girl. "Nothing's broken, I'm just a little... battered and bruised, that's all."

"What happened?"

"I'm still trying to figure that out," John admitted. "Call me crazy, but I'm getting the feeling that Sobolton's not quite..."

He paused as he tried to find the right word. At the same time, his gaze fell upon the forest on the lake's far side, and not for the first time he felt as if there was a huge amount he still didn't understand about his new home.

"You'll figure it out," Law said, patting him on the shoulder. "Most people round here have seen something odd from time to time. Something they can't explain. Most of us prefer to look away and hope that we're not disturbed too much. Did you see something last night, John? Something that perhaps doesn't sit right?"

"I saw..."

John paused yet again, thinking back to the sight of the twisted, monstrous creature that had launched such a furious attack.

"Apparently the lake's very deep in places," he said finally. "I'm advised that we don't really have the budget to trawl the depths, and that even if we did, we probably wouldn't find anything. I saw something last night that seemed... stuck between two worlds, as if..."

Again his voice trailed off. His impression

was that the creature had been half man and half wolf, and that something had halted its transformation from one form to the other; he'd briefly spotted something glinting in a wound on the creature's chest, and he couldn't help wondering whether a man had been on the verge of changing to become a wolf, only for some kind of metal to interrupt the process, leaving the wretched thing permanently stuck form that was neither one thing or another. He wasn't prone to such flights of fancy, and he certainly had no intention of making a fool of himself by voicing such fears, yet to his surprise he found himself unable to entirely dismiss such a crazy notion. And that realization, in turn, made him wonder whether he was losing his goddamn mind.

"Come and see me this afternoon," Law said finally. "By then I should have had time to get to the girl and make some initial assessments. Something tells me that we should really try to move with some pace on this investigation. Someone out there has to be missing a child."

"I couldn't agree more," John murmured. "I'd appreciate a swift job on this, Doctor Law. There has to be some reason why this girl ended up in the ice, and so far we don't even have a name." He watched as various deputies began to approach the block of ice, peering at the girl still trapped in its heart. "I'm going to find her name," he added, "and her family, and I'm going to make sure she can rest in peace."

"I'll do my absolute best," Law told him, and then it was his turn to pause for a few seconds. "And it's Robert, by the way. My name. You can call me Robert."

CHAPTER THIRTY

"THIS IS SO HARD for me to say," Wade uttered hesitantly over the phone, as Lisa stood outside the sheriff's office. "I wanted to tell you to your face, Lisa, I swear I did but -"

"Just spit it out," she replied, staring out across the parking lot as the garage tow truck brought her wrecked car back for repairs. "You're not coming home today, are you?"

"I didn't lie when I told you I had a lot of work to do," he continued. "I was telling you the truth about that, Lisa, I swear."

"What's her name?"

"Lisa, I -"

"What's her name, Wade?" she said firmly, cutting him off. Tears were welling in her eyes, although in truth – if she was honest with herself –

she'd been aware for a while that this whole fiasco might be coming. "Can't I at least know the name of the woman you're running off with?"

"Do you really want to do it like this?"

"Yes, actually," she told him, "I do. What's her name, Wade?"

She waited, but for a few seconds she heard no reply.

"Karen," he said nervously.

"Nice name," Lisa replied, before swallowing hard. "So what about your things? You've got some stuff in my apartment, I assume you'd like that back."

"Lisa -"

"I'll pack it up," she added, "and you can give me an address to ship it to. Just don't take too long, okay? I don't want it cluttering my place up, I'm already short of room as it is. If you leave it too long, I might just be tempted to take it all down to goodwill."

"What happened to you last night?" he asked. "You said there was something you wanted to tell me before I blurted all of this out. Despite everything that's happened between us, Lisa, I still value our friendship."

"Last night?" she replied, briefly considering telling him everything before realizing that she needed to make a clear break. "Nothing. Nothing I want to talk about, anyway. I just think this conversation needs to be over, and you can text me an address for sending your stuff, and then I don't think we need to have any more contact with each other."

"I don't want to leave things like this," he said firmly, his voice breaking up a little as the signal fluctuated. "I still think you're a great person. It's just that I've been away so much lately, and naturally I've been getting a little lonely and then Karen showed up in the office and we just sort of hit it off right away and -"

"I have to go," she told him, interrupting him before he could say more. "I wish you nothing but the best, Wade. Send me that address."

With that, before he could say more, she cut the call off and turned to hurry into the sheriff's office. As she pushed the door open she felt a buzz in her pocket; she checked her phone and saw that, sure enough, Wade had sent through an address for a place several states away, no doubt the home of this Karen woman. She briefly considered lugging his stuff down to goodwill anyway, before telling herself that she had to be the bigger person and not give him any ammunition.

As she approached the front desk, she sniffed back a few last remaining tears and told herself she could cry properly when she got home.

"Doctor Sondnes," Carolyn said, looking up at her with a rather forced smile, "to what do we owe the pleasure of this visit?"

"I need to see the new sheriff," Lisa replied. "Right now."

***

"This is just preliminary, of course," Law said, as he and John stood on either side of the examination table in a room at the back of the building, with the dead girl's sodden thawed body between them, "but so far the only wound I've found is this one on the back of her neck."

He used a pencil to indicate a bloodied patch just below her hairline.

"It's not deep," he continued, "and to be perfectly honest with you, I don't think it's the cause of death."

"If that didn't kill her," John replied, "then what did?"

"I must remind you that I haven't begun the autopsy yet," Law explained. "These are just initial observations. I wouldn't usually call the sheriff in at this stage, but I know you're keen to get as much information as you can, as soon as possible. She's still in quite a bad state, I've never conducted an autopsy on a body that's been frozen like this, but I'm hoping to proceed this afternoon. I must remind you, John, that she's only been out of the lake for a few hours. We're going to have to be a little patient for a little while longer, but I'm sure soon we'll get to the bottom of Little Miss Dead."

"Call me as soon as you know anything," John replied, turning and heading toward the door before stopping and glancing back at the doctor. "Wait, *what* did you just call her?"

"Who?" Law murmured, before sighing. "Oh, right. Sorry, it's just that what with her not having a name yet, I've been mentally using the phrase people have come up with in town."

"Little Miss Dead?"

"Stupid, right?"

"What people have been using that name?"

"It seems to have stuck," Law told him, and then he sighed again. "I know you were hoping to keep this under wraps until you had some more information, but that strategy's never going to work in a close-knit place like Sobolton. Joe Hicks has been shooting his mouth off, for one thing, plus all the deputies have families and you can't expect them not to talk."

"So the whole town's talking about this girl?"

"A few of the more impressionable types have even claimed to have seen the young girl hanging around, like a kind of ghost. Obviously I don't believe that for one second, but... People have a right to be worried, John."

"I know," John replied, nodding gently. "I

know, I wasn't trying to hide anything. I guess I just wanted to get ahead of the case a little and have some kind of positive news to share."

"People understand that you're not a miracle-worker," Law said firmly. "They won't be expecting you to solve this case by lunchtime." He paused yet again, before looking down at the dead girl on his table. "But don't take *too* long, John," he added cautiously. "People won't like it if this case drags on, especially seeing as how she's just a child. I don't know how long you've got, but you being new around these parts won't exactly help either."

"I need to prove myself," John murmured. "I'm fully aware of that fact."

"I'll do the best I can with the autopsy," Law continued, "and I'll have some thoughts for you by mid-afternoon. I'm on your side, John. We all are. And like you said, this girl *has* to have a name and a family and a story. We're going to figure it all out eventually."

"I know we are," John said, stepping out into the corridor and then watching the girl for a moment. "We have to."

He saw Law getting some equipment from a nearby counter, and then he let the door bump shut. Feeling exhausted and sore and more than a little injured, John began to make his way through to the front of the building. He knew he should get himself to the hospital for at least a brief check-up, but he figured there was no time for that just yet, not when he had to devote every spare second to the case. If people in town were talking, and if they'd already come up with this Little Miss Dead moniker, than he reckoned he was already running out of time and that soon the locals would run out of patience. A breakthrough had to be made, and fast.

Reaching the front desk, he saw a pile of folders resting on the side.

"Are these for me?" he asked Carolyn.

"That's everything I could find that fits what you asked about."

John took a moment to sort through the folders, before pulling one out and taking a moment to scan the report.

"Wolves," he murmured, feeling a flicker of recognition. "Possible... creatures?"

"Yeah," Carolyn said cautiously, "that one -"

"Sondnes," he continued, looking at the name at the bottom of the report. "Doctor Lisa Sondnes. A veterinarian. Sounds like someone who should know what she's talking about. I wouldn't have thought that a veterinarian would be given to misidentifying things and crying wolf. Pardon the pun."

Carolyn opened her mouth to reply, before looking over at the chairs in the corner. She saw Lisa sitting tapping at her phone; a moment later, as if she'd been lost in her thoughts, Lisa wiped away a stray tear and slipped her phone into her pocket, and then Carolyn watched as she got to her feet and made her way over to the desk, finally stopping right next to John.

"This is something I need to follow up," John said, turning the report around so that Carolyn could see the details. "I need to talk to this Doctor Lisa Sondnes woman immediately."

"Right," Carolyn replied, "but -"

"Can you get her on the phone for me?" John continued. "Or better still, can you tell me where I might find her?"

Carolyn opened her mouth again, but she hesitated as she stared at John for a moment and then turned to look at Lisa standing right next to him. And then, as the first tears reached her eyes, Carolyn watched as Lisa faded away into thin air.

"Well?" John said after a moment. "Can you get me in touch with Doctor Lisa Sondnes?"

"Nothing would give me greater pleasure," Carolyn replied, struggling to hold back tears, "but... Sir, Lisa Sondnes brought her report to this office twenty years ago. I remember that day almost as if it was yesterday." She paused, struggling to keep from breaking down completely. "She handed it in shortly before she disappeared."

AMY CROSS

THE HORRORS OF SOBOLTON

1. Little Miss Dead
2. Swan Territory
3. Dead Widow Road

More titles coming soon!

Next in this series

SWAN TERRITORY
(THE HORRORS OF SOBOLTON BOOK 2)

Many years ago, reclusive millionaire Wentworth Stone retreated from the world, seemingly unable to get over the death of his wife. Nobody has heard from him since... until the day he asks for help from Sobolton veterinarian Lisa Sondnes.

Heading out to Stone's remote home, Lisa discovers a flock of sick and diseased swans. Stone insists that they must be saved, but the more she tries to treat the birds, the more Lisa starts to wonder whether they might be hiding a strange secret. When she discovers a hidden cave on Stone's property, she realizes that her worst fears are about to come true.

Meanwhile, John investigates a mystery of his own, one that's clearly linked to a tragedy that occurred many years ago. Wentworth Stone's crumbling mansion hides a second secret, one that threatens to burst back into the world just as a ghostly little girl makes her second appearance.

Also by Amy Cross

1689
(The Haunting of Hadlow House book 1)

All Richard Hadlow wants is a happy family and a peaceful home. Having built the perfect house deep in the Kent countryside, now all he needs is a wife. He's about to discover, however, that even the most perfectly-laid plans can go horribly and tragically wrong.

The year is 1689 and England is in the grip of turmoil. A pretender is trying to take the throne, but Richard has no interest in the affairs of his country. He only cares about finding the perfect wife and giving her a perfect life. But someone – or something – at his newly-built house has other ideas. Is Richard's new life about to be destroyed forever?

Hadlow House is brand new, but already there are strange whispers in the corridors and unexplained noises at night. Has Richard been unlucky, is his new wife simply imagining things, or is a dark secret from the past about to rise up and deliver Richard's worst nightmare? Who wins when the past and the present collide?

AMY CROSS

LITTLE MISS DEAD

Also by Amy Cross

The Haunting of Nelson Street (The Ghosts of Crowford book 1)

Crowford, a sleepy coastal town in the south of England, might seem like an oasis of calm and tranquility. Beneath the surface, however, dark secrets are waiting to claim fresh victims, and ghostly figures plot revenge.

Having finally decided to leave the hustle of London, Daisy and Richard Johnson buy two houses on Nelson Street, a picturesque street in the center of Crowford. One house is perfect and ready to move into, while the other is a fire-ravaged wreck that needs a lot of work. They figure they have plenty of time to work on the damaged house while Daisy recovers from a traumatic event.

Soon, they discover that the two houses share a common link to the past. Something awful once happened on Nelson Street, something that shook the town to its core.

Also by Amy Cross

**The Revenge of the Mercy Belle
(The Ghosts of Crowford book 2)**

The year is 1950, and a great tragedy has struck the town of Crowford. Three local men have been killed in a storm, after their fishing boat the Mercy Belle sank. A mysterious fourth man, however, was rescue. Nobody knows who he is, or what he was doing on the Mercy Belle... and the man has lost his memory.

Five years later, messages from the dead warn of impending doom for Crowford. The ghosts of the Mercy Belle's crew demand revenge, and the whole town is being punished. The fourth man still has no memory of his previous existence, but he's married now and living under the named Edward Smith. As Crowford's suffering continues, the locals begin to turn against him.

What really happened on the night the Mercy Belle sank? Did the fourth man cause the tragedy? And will Crowford survive if this man is not sent to meet his fate?

AMY CROSS

Also by Amy Cross

The Devil, the Witch and the Whore (The Deal book 1)

"Leave the forest alone. Whatever's out there, just let it be. Don't make it angry."

When a horrific discovery is made at the edge of town, Sheriff James Kopperud realizes the answers he seeks might be waiting beyond in the vast forest. But everybody in the town of Deal knows that there's something out there in the forest, something that should never be disturbed. A deal was made long ago, a deal that was supposed to keep the town safe. And if he insists on investigating the murder of a local girl, James is going to have to break that deal and head out into the wilderness.

Meanwhile, James has no idea that his estranged daughter Ramsey has returned to town. Ramsey is running from something, and she thinks she can find safety in the vast tunnel system that runs beneath the forest. Before long, however, Ramsey finds herself coming face to face with creatures that hide in the shadows. One of these creatures is known as the devil, and another is known as the witch. They're both waiting for the whore to arrive, but for very different reasons. And soon Ramsey is offered a terrible deal, one that could save or destroy the entire town, and maybe even the world.

AMY CROSS

Also by Amy Cross

The Soul Auction

"I saw a woman on the beach. I watched her face a demon."

Thirty years after her mother's death, Alice Ashcroft is drawn back to the coastal English town of Curridge. Somebody in Curridge has been reviewing Alice's novels online, and in those reviews there have been tantalizing hints at a hidden truth. A truth that seems to be linked to her dead mother.

"Thirty years ago, there was a soul auction."

Once she reaches Curridge, Alice finds strange things happening all around her. Something attacks her car. A figure watches her on the beach at night. And when she tries to find the person who has been reviewing her books, she makes a horrific discovery.

What really happened to Alice's mother thirty years ago? Who was she talking to, just moments before dropping dead on the beach? What caused a huge rockfall that nearly tore a nearby cliff-face in half? And what sinister presence is lurking in the grounds of the local church?

AMY CROSS

Also by Amy Cross

The Haunting of Hurst House (Mercy Willow book 1)

When she moves to a small coastal Cornish village, Mercy Willow hopes to start a new life. She has a brand new job as an estate agent, and she's determined to put the past where it belongs and get on with building a new future. But will that be easy in a village that has more than its fair share of ghosts?

Determined to sell the un-sellable Hurst House, Mercy gets straight to work. Hurst House was once the scene of a terrible tragedy, and many of the locals believe that the place is best left untouched and undisturbed. Mercy, however, thinks it just needs a lick of paint and a few other improvements, and that then she'll be able to find a buyer in no time.

Soon, Mercy discovers that parts of Hurst House's past are still lingering. Strange noises hint at an unseen presence, and an old family secret is about to come bursting back to life with terrifying consequences. Meanwhile, Mercy herself has a dark past that she'd rather keep hidden. After all, her name isn't really Mercy Willow at all, and she's running from something that has already almost killed her once.

AMY CROSS

Also by Amy Cross

Darper Danver: The Complete First Series

Five years ago, three friends went to a remote cabin in the woods and tried to contact the spirit of a long-dead soldier. They thought they could control whatever happened next. They were wrong...

Newly released from prison, Cassie Briggs returns to Fort Powell, determined to get her life back on track. Soon, however, she begins to suspect that an ancient evil still lurks in the nearby cabin. Was the mysterious Darper Danver really destroyed all those years ago, or does her spirit still linger, waiting for a chance to return?

As Cassie and her ex-boyfriend Fisher are finally forced to face the truth about what happened in the cabin, they realize that Darper isn't ready to let go of their lives just yet. Meanwhile, a vengeful woman plots revenge for her brother's murder, and a New York ghost writer arrives in town to uncover the truth. Before long, strange carvings begin to appear around town and blood starts to flow once again.

AMY CROSS

Also by Amy Cross

The Ghost of Molly Holt

"Molly Holt is dead. There's nothing to fear in this house."

When three teenagers set out to explore an abandoned house in the middle of a forest, they think they've found the location where the infamous Molly Holt video was filmed.

They've found much more than that...

Tim doesn't believe in ghosts, but he has a crush on a girl who does. That's why he ends up taking her out to the house, and it's also why he lets her take his only flashlight. But as they explore the house together, Tim and Becky start to realize that something else might be lurking in the shadows.

Something that, ten years ago, suffered unimaginable pain.

Something that won't rest until a terrible wrong has been put right.

Also by Amy Cross

American Coven

He kidnapped three women and held them in his basement. He thought they couldn't fight back. He was wrong...

Snatched from the street near her home, Holly Carter is taken to a rural house and thrown down into a stone basement. She meets two other women who have also been kidnapped, and soon Holly learns about the horrific rituals that take place in the house. Eventually, she's called upstairs to take her place in the ice bath.

As her nightmare continues, however, Holly learns about a mysterious power that exists in the basement, and which the three women might be able to harness. When they finally manage to get through the metal door, however, the women have no idea that their fight for freedom is going to stretch out for more than a decade, or that it will culminate in a final, devastating demonstration of their new-found powers.

AMY CROSS

LITTLE MISS DEAD

Also by Amy Cross

The Ash House

Why would anyone ever return to a haunted house?

For Diane Mercer the answer is simple. She's dying of cancer, and she wants to know once and for all whether ghosts are real.

Heading home with her young son, Diane is determined to find out whether the stories are real. After all, everyone else claimed to see and hear strange things in the house over the years. Everyone except Diane had some kind of experience in the house, or in the little ash house in the yard.

As Diane explores the house where she grew up, however, her son is exploring the yard and the forest. And while his mother might be struggling to come to terms with her own impending death, Daniel Mercer is puzzled by fleeting appearances of a strange little girl who seems drawn to the ash house, and by strange, rasping coughs that he keeps hearing at night.

The Ash House is a horror novel about a woman who desperately wants to know what will happen to her when she dies, and about a boy who uncovers the shocking truth about a young girl's murder.

Also by Amy Cross

Haunted

Twenty years ago, the ghost of a dead little girl drove Sheriff Michael Blaine to his death.

Now, that same ghost is coming for his daughter.

Returning to the small town where she grew up, Alex Roberts is determined to live a normal, quiet life. For the residents of Railham, however, she's an unwelcome reminder of the town's darkest hour.

Twenty years ago, nine-year-old Mo Garvey was found brutally murdered in a nearby forest. Everyone thinks that Alex's father was responsible, but if the killer was brought to justice, why is the ghost of Mo Garvey still after revenge?

And how far will the real killer go to protect his secret, when Alex starts getting closer to the truth?

Haunted is a horror novel about a woman who has to face her past, about a town that would rather forget, and about a little girl who refuses to let death stand in her way.

AMY CROSS

Also by Amy Cross

The Curse of Wetherley House

"If you walk through that door, Evil Mary will get you."

When she agrees to visit a supposedly haunted house with an old friend, Rosie assumes she'll encounter nothing more scary than a few creaks and bumps in the night. Even the legend of Evil Mary doesn't put her off. After all, she knows ghosts aren't real. But when Mary makes her first appearance, Rosie realizes she might already be trapped.

For more than a century, Wetherley House has been cursed. A horrific encounter on a remote road in the late 1800's has already caused a chain of misery and pain for all those who live at the house. Wetherley House was abandoned long ago, after a terrible discovery in the basement, something has remained undetected within its room. And even the local children know that Evil Mary waits in the house for anyone foolish enough to walk through the front door.

Before long, Rosie realizes that her entire life has been defined by the spirit of a woman who died in agony. Can she become the first person to escape Evil Mary, or will she fall victim to the same fate as the house's other occupants?

AMY CROSS

Also by Amy Cross

The Girl Who Never Came Back

Twenty years ago, Charlotte Abernathy vanished while playing near her family's house. Despite a frantic search, no trace of her was found until a year later, when the little girl turned up on the doorstep with no memory of where she'd been.

Today, Charlotte has put her mysterious ordeal behind her, even though she's never learned where she was during that missing year. However, when her eight-year-old niece vanishes in similar circumstances, a fully-grown Charlotte is forced to make a fresh attempt to uncover the truth.

Originally published in 2013, the fully revised and updated version of *The Girl Who Never Came Back* tells the harrowing story of a woman who thought she could forget her past, and of a little girl caught in the tangled web of a dark family secret.

AMY CROSS

BOOKS BY AMY CROSS

1. Dark Season: The Complete First Series (2011)
2. Werewolves of Soho (Lupine Howl book 1) (2012)
3. Werewolves of the Other London (Lupine Howl book 2) (2012)
4. Ghosts: The Complete Series (2012)
5. Dark Season: The Complete Second Series (2012)
6. The Children of Black Annis (Lupine Howl book 3) (2012)
7. Destiny of the Last Wolf (Lupine Howl book 4) (2012)
8. Asylum (The Asylum Trilogy book 1) (2012)
9. Dark Season: The Complete Third Series (2013)
10. Devil's Briar (2013)
11. Broken Blue (The Broken Trilogy book 1) (2013)
12. The Night Girl (2013)
13. Days 1 to 4 (Mass Extinction Event book 1) (2013)
14. Days 5 to 8 (Mass Extinction Event book 2) (2013)
15. The Library (The Library Chronicles book 1) (2013)
16. American Coven (2013)
17. Werewolves of Sangreth (Lupine Howl book 5) (2013)
18. Broken White (The Broken Trilogy book 2) (2013)
19. Grave Girl (Grave Girl book 1) (2013)
20. Other People's Bodies (2013)
21. The Shades (2013)
22. The Vampire's Grave and Other Stories (2013)
23. Darper Danver: The Complete First Series (2013)
24. The Hollow Church (2013)
25. The Dead and the Dying (2013)
26. Days 9 to 16 (Mass Extinction Event book 3) (2013)
27. The Girl Who Never Came Back (2013)
28. Ward Z (The Ward Z Series book 1) (2013)
29. Journey to the Library (The Library Chronicles book 2) (2014)
30. The Vampires of Tor Cliff Asylum (2014)
31. The Family Man (2014)
32. The Devil's Blade (2014)
33. The Immortal Wolf (Lupine Howl book 6) (2014)
34. The Dying Streets (Detective Laura Foster book 1) (2014)
35. The Stars My Home (2014)
36. The Ghost in the Rain and Other Stories (2014)
37. Ghosts of the River Thames (The Robinson Chronicles book 1) (2014)
38. The Wolves of Cur'eath (2014)
39. Days 46 to 53 (Mass Extinction Event book 4) (2014)
40. The Man Who Saw the Face of the World (2014)
41. The Art of Dying (Detective Laura Foster book 2) (2014)
42. Raven Revivals (Grave Girl book 2) (2014)

AMY CROSS

43. Arrival on Thaxos (Dead Souls book 1) (2014)
44. Birthright (Dead Souls book 2) (2014)
45. A Man of Ghosts (Dead Souls book 3) (2014)
46. The Haunting of Hardstone Jail (2014)
47. A Very Respectable Woman (2015)
48. Better the Devil (2015)
49. The Haunting of Marshall Heights (2015)
50. Terror at Camp Everbee (The Ward Z Series book 2) (2015)
51. Guided by Evil (Dead Souls book 4) (2015)
52. Child of a Bloodied Hand (Dead Souls book 5) (2015)
53. Promises of the Dead (Dead Souls book 6) (2015)
54. Days 54 to 61 (Mass Extinction Event book 5) (2015)
55. Angels in the Machine (The Robinson Chronicles book 2) (2015)
56. The Curse of Ah-Qal's Tomb (2015)
57. Broken Red (The Broken Trilogy book 3) (2015)
58. The Farm (2015)
59. Fallen Heroes (Detective Laura Foster book 3) (2015)
60. The Haunting of Emily Stone (2015)
61. Cursed Across Time (Dead Souls book 7) (2015)
62. Destiny of the Dead (Dead Souls book 8) (2015)
63. The Death of Jennifer Kazakos (Dead Souls book 9) (2015)
64. Alice Isn't Well (Death Herself book 1) (2015)
65. Annie's Room (2015)
66. The House on Everley Street (Death Herself book 2) (2015)
67. Meds (The Asylum Trilogy book 2) (2015)
68. Take Me to Church (2015)
69. Ascension (Demon's Grail book 1) (2015)
70. The Priest Hole (Nykolas Freeman book 1) (2015)
71. Eli's Town (2015)
72. The Horror of Raven's Briar Orphanage (Dead Souls book 10) (2015)
73. The Witch of Thaxos (Dead Souls book 11) (2015)
74. The Rise of Ashalla (Dead Souls book 12) (2015)
75. Evolution (Demon's Grail book 2) (2015)
76. The Island (The Island book 1) (2015)
77. The Lighthouse (2015)
78. The Cabin (The Cabin Trilogy book 1) (2015)
79. At the Edge of the Forest (2015)
80. The Devil's Hand (2015)
81. The 13th Demon (Demon's Grail book 3) (2016)
82. After the Cabin (The Cabin Trilogy book 2) (2016)
83. The Border: The Complete Series (2016)
84. The Dead Ones (Death Herself book 3) (2016)
85. A House in London (2016)
86. Persona (The Island book 2) (2016)

87. Battlefield (Nykolas Freeman book 2) (2016)
88. Perfect Little Monsters and Other Stories (2016)
89. The Ghost of Shapley Hall (2016)
90. The Blood House (2016)
91. The Death of Addie Gray (2016)
92. The Girl With Crooked Fangs (2016)
93. Last Wrong Turn (2016)
94. The Body at Auercliff (2016)
95. The Printer From Hell (2016)
96. The Dog (2016)
97. The Nurse (2016)
98. The Haunting of Blackwych Grange (2016)
99. Twisted Little Things and Other Stories (2016)
100. The Horror of Devil's Root Lake (2016)
101. The Disappearance of Katie Wren (2016)
102. B&B (2016)
103. The Bride of Ashbyrn House (2016)
104. The Devil, the Witch and the Whore (The Deal Trilogy book 1) (2016)
105. The Ghosts of Lakeforth Hotel (2016)
106. The Ghost of Longthorn Manor and Other Stories (2016)
107. Laura (2017)
108. The Murder at Skellin Cottage (Jo Mason book 1) (2017)
109. The Curse of Wetherley House (2017)
110. The Ghosts of Hexley Airport (2017)
111. The Return of Rachel Stone (Jo Mason book 2) (2017)
112. Haunted (2017)
113. The Vampire of Downing Street and Other Stories (2017)
114. The Ash House (2017)
115. The Ghost of Molly Holt (2017)
116. The Camera Man (2017)
117. The Soul Auction (2017)
118. The Abyss (The Island book 3) (2017)
119. Broken Window (The House of Jack the Ripper book 1) (2017)
120. In Darkness Dwell (The House of Jack the Ripper book 2) (2017)
121. Cradle to Grave (The House of Jack the Ripper book 3) (2017)
122. The Lady Screams (The House of Jack the Ripper book 4) (2017)
123. A Beast Well Tamed (The House of Jack the Ripper book 5) (2017)
124. Doctor Charles Grazier (The House of Jack the Ripper book 6) (2017)
125. The Raven Watcher (The House of Jack the Ripper book 7) (2017)
126. The Final Act (The House of Jack the Ripper book 8) (2017)
127. Stephen (2017)
128. The Spider (2017)
129. The Mermaid's Revenge (2017)
130. The Girl Who Threw Rocks at the Devil (2018)

AMY CROSS

131. Friend From the Internet (2018)
132. Beautiful Familiar (2018)
133. One Night at a Soul Auction (2018)
134. 16 Frames of the Devil's Face (2018)
135. The Haunting of Caldgrave House (2018)
136. Like Stones on a Crow's Back (The Deal Trilogy book 2) (2018)
137. Room 9 and Other Stories (2018)
138. The Gravest Girl of All (Grave Girl book 3) (2018)
139. Return to Thaxos (Dead Souls book 13) (2018)
140. The Madness of Annie Radford (The Asylum Trilogy book 3) (2018)
141. The Haunting of Briarwych Church (Briarwych book 1) (2018)
142. I Just Want You To Be Happy (2018)
143. Day 100 (Mass Extinction Event book 6) (2018)
144. The Horror of Briarwych Church (Briarwych book 2) (2018)
145. The Ghost of Briarwych Church (Briarwych book 3) (2018)
146. Lights Out (2019)
147. Apocalypse (The Ward Z Series book 3) (2019)
148. Days 101 to 108 (Mass Extinction Event book 7) (2019)
149. The Haunting of Daniel Bayliss (2019)
150. The Purchase (2019)
151. Harper's Hotel Ghost Girl (Death Herself book 4) (2019)
152. The Haunting of Aldburn House (2019)
153. Days 109 to 116 (Mass Extinction Event book 8) (2019)
154. Bad News (2019)
155. The Wedding of Rachel Blaine (2019)
156. Dark Little Wonders and Other Stories (2019)
157. The Music Man (2019)
158. The Vampire Falls (Three Nights of the Vampire book 1) (2019)
159. The Other Ann (2019)
160. The Butcher's Husband and Other Stories (2019)
161. The Haunting of Lannister Hall (2019)
162. The Vampire Burns (Three Nights of the Vampire book 2) (2019)
163. Days 195 to 202 (Mass Extinction Event book 9) (2019)
164. Escape From Hotel Necro (2019)
165. The Vampire Rises (Three Nights of the Vampire book 3) (2019)
166. Ten Chimes to Midnight: A Collection of Ghost Stories (2019)
167. The Strangler's Daughter (2019)
168. The Beast on the Tracks (2019)
169. The Haunting of the King's Head (2019)
170. I Married a Serial Killer (2019)
171. Your Inhuman Heart (2020)
172. Days 203 to 210 (Mass Extinction Event book 10) (2020)
173. The Ghosts of David Brook (2020)
174. Days 349 to 356 (Mass Extinction Event book 11) (2020)

175. The Horror at Criven Farm (2020)
176. Mary (2020)
177. The Middlewych Experiment (Chaos Gear Annie book 1) (2020)
178. Days 357 to 364 (Mass Extinction Event book 12) (2020)
179. Day 365: The Final Day (Mass Extinction Event book 13) (2020)
180. The Haunting of Hathaway House (2020)
181. Don't Let the Devil Know Your Name (2020)
182. The Legend of Rinth (2020)
183. The Ghost of Old Coal House (2020)
184. The Root (2020)
185. I'm Not a Zombie (2020)
186. The Ghost of Annie Close (2020)
187. The Disappearance of Lonnie James (2020)
188. The Curse of the Langfords (2020)
189. The Haunting of Nelson Street (The Ghosts of Crowford 1) (2020)
190. Strange Little Horrors and Other Stories (2020)
191. The House Where She Died (2020)
192. The Revenge of the Mercy Belle (The Ghosts of Crowford 2) (2020)
193. The Ghost of Crowford School (The Ghosts of Crowford book 3) (2020)
194. The Haunting of Hardlocke House (2020)
195. The Cemetery Ghost (2020)
196. You Should Have Seen Her (2020)
197. The Portrait of Sister Elsa (The Ghosts of Crowford book 4) (2021)
198. The House on Fisher Street (2021)
199. The Haunting of the Crowford Hoy (The Ghosts of Crowford 5) (2021)
200. Trill (2021)
201. The Horror of the Crowford Empire (The Ghosts of Crowford 6) (2021)
202. Out There (The Ted Armitage Trilogy book 1) (2021)
203. The Nightmare of Crowford Hospital (The Ghosts of Crowford 7) (2021)
204. Twist Valley (The Ted Armitage Trilogy book 2) (2021)
205. The Great Beyond (The Ted Armitage Trilogy book 3) (2021)
206. The Haunting of Edward House (2021)
207. The Curse of the Crowford Grand (The Ghosts of Crowford 8) (2021)
208. How to Make a Ghost (2021)
209. The Ghosts of Crossley Manor (The Ghosts of Crowford 9) (2021)
210. The Haunting of Matthew Thorne (2021)
211. The Siege of Crowford Castle (The Ghosts of Crowford 10) (2021)
212. Daisy: The Complete Series (2021)
213. Bait (Bait book 1) (2021)
214. Origin (Bait book 2) (2021)
215. Heretic (Bait book 3) (2021)
216. Anna's Sister (2021)
217. The Haunting of Quist House (The Rose Files 1) (2021)
218. The Haunting of Crowford Station (The Ghosts of Crowford 11) (2022)

AMY CROSS

219. The Curse of Rosie Stone (2022)
220. The First Order (The Chronicles of Sister June book 1) (2022)
221. The Second Veil (The Chronicles of Sister June book 2) (2022)
222. The Graves of Crowford Rise (The Ghosts of Crowford 12) (2022)
223. Dead Man: The Resurrection of Morton Kane (2022)
224. The Third Beast (The Chronicles of Sister June book 3) (2022)
225. The Legend of the Crossley Stag (The Ghosts of Crowford 13) (2022)
226. One Star (2022)
227. The Ghost in Room 119 (2022)
228. The Fourth Shadow (The Chronicles of Sister June book 4) (2022)
229. The Soldier Without a Past (Dead Souls book 14) (2022)
230. The Ghosts of Marsh House (2022)
231. Wax: The Complete Series (2022)
232. The Phantom of Crowford Theatre (The Ghosts of Crowford 14) (2022)
233. The Haunting of Hurst House (Mercy Willow book 1) (2022)
234. Blood Rains Down From the Sky (The Deal Trilogy book 3) (2022)
235. The Spirit on Sidle Street (Mercy Willow book 2) (2022)
236. The Ghost of Gower Grange (Mercy Willow book 3) (2022)
237. The Curse of Clute Cottage (Mercy Willow book 4) (2022)
238. The Haunting of Anna Jenkins (Mercy Willow book 5) (2023)
239. The Death of Mercy Willow (Mercy Willow book 6) (2023)
240. Angel (2023)
241. The Eyes of Maddy Park (2023)
242. If You Didn't Like Me Then, You Probably Won't Like Me Now (2023)
243. The Terror of Torfork Tower (Mercy Willow 7) (2023)
244. The Phantom of Payne Priory (Mercy Willow 8) (2023)
245. The Devil on Davis Drive (Mercy Willow 9) (2023)
246. The Haunting of the Ghost of Tom Bell (Mercy Willow 10) (2023)
247. The Other Ghost of Gower Grange (Mercy Willow 11) (2023)
248. The Haunting of Olive Atkins (Mercy Willow 12) (2023)
249. The End of Marcy Willow (Mercy Willow 13) (2023)
250. The Last Haunted House on Mars and Other Stories (2023)
251. 1689 (The Haunting of Hadlow House 1) (2023)
252. 1722 (The Haunting of Hadlow House 2) (2023)
253. 1775 (The Haunting of Hadlow House 3) (2023)
254. The Terror of Crowford Carnival (The Ghosts of Crowford 15) (2023)
255. 1800 (The Haunting of Hadlow House 4) (2023)
256. 1837 (The Haunting of Hadlow House 5) (2023)
257. 1885 (The Haunting of Hadlow House 6) (2023)
258. 1901 (The Haunting of Hadlow House 7) (2023)
259. 1918 (The Haunting of Hadlow House 8) (2023)
260. The Secret of Adam Grey (The Ghosts of Crowford 16) (2023)
261. 1926 (The Haunting of Hadlow House 9) (2023)
262. 1939 (The Haunting of Hadlow House 10) (2023)

263. The Fifth Tomb (The Chronicles of Sister June 5) (2023)
264. 1966 (The Haunting of Hadlow House 11) (2023)
265. 1999 (The Haunting of Hadlow House 12) (2023)
266. The Hauntings of Mia Rush (2023)
267. 2024 (The Haunting of Hadlow House 13) (2024)
268. The Sixth Window (The Chronicles of Sister June 6) (2024)
269. Little Miss Dead (The Horrors of Sobolton 1) (2024)

AMY CROSS

For more information, visit:

www.amycross.com

AMY CROSS